VIKING'S BRIDE
CALLED BY A VIKING
BOOK THREE

MARIAH STONE

Stone Publishing

This is a work of fiction. Names, characters, places, and incidents either are the products of the author's imagination or are used fictitiously. Any resemblance to actual persons, living or dead, businesses, companies, events, or locales is entirely coincidental.

© 2019 "The Marriage of Time" Mariah Stone. All rights reserved.

© 2023 "Viking's Bride" Mariah Stone. All rights reserved.

Cover design by Qamber Designs and Media

All rights reserved. This book or parts thereof may not be reproduced in any form, stored in any retrieval system, or transmitted in any form by any means—electronic, mechanical, photocopy, recording, or otherwise—without prior written permission of the publisher. For permission requests, contact the publisher at http:\\mariahstone.com

GET A FREE MARIAH STONE BOOK!

Join Mariah's mailing list to be the first to know of new releases, free books, special prices, and other author giveaways.

freehistoricalromancebooks.com

Also by Mariah Stone

MARIAH'S TIME TRAVEL ROMANCE SERIES

- Called by a Highlander
- Called by a Viking
- Called by a Pirate
- Fated

MARIAH'S REGENCY ROMANCE SERIES

- Dukes and Secrets

VIEW ALL OF MARIAH'S BOOKS IN READING ORDER

Scan the QR code for the complete list of Mariah's ebooks, paperbacks, and audiobooks in reading order.

To all medical professionals

PROLOGUE

SOMEWHERE IN ROGALAND, Norway, October 15, 874 AD

THE SCENT of blood was so thick Hakon tasted iron on his tongue. Swords and axes thumped against wooden shields. Screams rang through the air as metal pierced flesh and bone.

His men were falling. He was losing.

Hakon stabbed the tattooed warrior under the ribs with his scramasax, kicked another one in the stomach, then whirled and drove his battle ax into the chest of the third one.

King Nyr sat on his horse across the clearing where their forces clashed, woods and mountains surrounding them. He watched Hakon with a triumphant sneer.

Rage ignited within Hakon, giving him power. He was the lightning that struck the tree. He was the spear that pierced the elk.

He was Thor's hammer.

He was vengeance itself.

And King Nyr was his target.

One after another, men fell under Hakon's ax, but he saw only King Nyr. The men fighting around him were flashes of hair, muscle, and iron.

Finally, Nyr was in front of him. He'd throw the man off his horse and drive his ax through the bastard's heart. But as he tensed his muscles to lunge forward, his body slowed and stopped. His limbs were weighed down as if he had sunk into a swamp.

He looked around. Men.

They held him, their eyes round, their eyebrows snapped together. Nyr sat high and proud on his horse, eyeing him from above. His bald head, with its dark, shadowed eyes, looked like a skull.

Hakon roared and jerked with all his might. Like Fenrir, the giant wolf bound by unbreakable chains, he fought and bit, teeth gnashing, claws flashing. But he could not get free.

"They say you are unstoppable, Beast," Nyr said. "I see that it is not true."

Hakon gritted his teeth. "Thor, give me your hammer to strike this snake."

"Why so hostile, Hakon? Your father and I were friends."

"I remember. *Friend*. I remember your visit sixteen winters ago, the freezing night my mother took me into the woods after a blizzard. I remember the traces of the wolf pack in the snow after they followed her horse away from me. And I remember the remnants of her body after they tore her apart. I have asked myself over and over, why she suddenly decided to take me to her family that night. Why she insisted it was no longer safe at home. Now I know. It was because of you."

Nyr's face straightened and paled as he listened. "You know?"

Hakon nodded. "My father told me on his death bed two years ago. You suggested he let the gods test my curse."

Hakon's left eye—the one with a birthmark around it—twitched. "She died because of your wicked scheme. You took the dearest person in the world from me. And now it is time to pay. The Beast has come for you."

Nyr's throat bobbed under his short white beard. "I am growing weary of your rage, Hakon. I never intended for your mother to die, and I never intended for us to be enemies. Be my ally. I want you by my side."

A low, animal growl escaped Hakon's throat. Fury was burning his gut like hot vinegar. Be his ally? Give up? Never. He had lost the battle, but not the war.

Nyr's chin rose. "First choice, you die. You, your men, and every single person in your village. Your lands become mine—something I have wanted for a long time. But I do not wish your death. I want the Beast on my side. I want you to fight for me like you have fought against me. Second choice, you become my kinsman."

The urge for revenge made his hands itch and burn as if he had just rubbed his palms in nettle. He growled again, a mixture of laughter and threat. He would never be kin to this monster.

"You were robbed of your mother." Nyr lifted one shoulder. "Let me give you another woman who would love you. Marry my daughter."

Hakon froze. "What?"

"I have nine girls and no boys. My daughters' task is to bring me the sons and alliances I need."

Hakon could not believe what the worm was suggesting.

"Become my son-in-law." Nyr tilted his head back slightly. "You will keep your lands and pay me tribute as your king. You will protect me if I need your warriors, and you will back me at the assembly, the *Thing*. What say you?"

"Have your *brat* for a wife?" Hakon spat. "What Loki's plan is this?"

He could not have a wife. Not the least the daughter of his enemy.

"I am not jesting."

"Do you hate your daughter so much that you will marry her to the Beast?" Hakon heard the thunder in his own voice.

Nyr did not even twitch. "Do you not want a family?"

Hakon had abandoned the hope of having a normal life long ago. "You said that I was cursed. Are you not afraid your daughter will be cursed, as well?"

Nyr chuckled. "I have so many, nothing will change if a little curse comes to this one."

Hakon watched Nyr from under his heavy lids. He felt as if he were caught in a trap, looking for a way out.

And he had found one. Nyr had just given Hakon a way to destroy him. Loki must have sat on his shoulder and whispered a scheme. A truly cunning scheme.

All Hakon needed were allies with more men. Marrying Nyr's daughter would be the best way to make connections while gaining his enemy's trust. Hakon straightened, his shoulders relaxed. His fury still thundered in his stomach, but it had taken a form.

The form of a spear.

"Marry your daughter, you say?"

"Yes. My daughter, Arinborg. She's the next one of marrying age."

Hakon did not care if she was an old woman. It would not be a true marriage anyway. "How do I know that you will leave us alone?"

Nyr cocked his head. "I give you my word."

Hakon laughed. "Your word. Your word is like spitting into a fjord. It means nothing."

Nyr's eyes darkened. "What do you want as a guarantee?"

Hakon narrowed his eyes. Nyr could use his daughter as a spy. The only way to avoid that was to isolate her from her kinsmen. She needed to be completely under Hakon's control. "Let her come alone. No one will accompany her. No one will attend the wedding. If she comes alone, I will take it as the sign of peace. If I hear a twig break near her, she'll die before her heart can take its next beat."

Nyr's jaw moved from side to side. "The way is long. Winter is upon us. Let it be next summer solstice. She will be there, alone."

Triumph spread in Hakon's stomach like warmth from a hot stone. "The day of summer solstice. There is a sacred grove with a rune stone up the mountain by my village. I will wait for her there."

"Let it be so, Beast. Send word when the thing is done."

Hakon gave a curt nod. Nyr gestured, and the men let go of Hakon. His jaw tightened. Now that he was free, he itched for his ax, for a chance to kill Nyr.

Nyr's men began retreating into the woods, and the king turned his horse away and rode off.

Hakon's fists clenched and unclenched, gripping empty air. He had agreed to marry Nyr's daughter, to become *mágr* to the man who had caused his mother's death. Was he mad?

Hakon's birthmark burned, reminding him of his curse.

He would need to keep his distance from his future wife—she would surely spy on him, even if he did keep her away from her kin. But at least he need not worry about developing feelings for the daughter of his enemy.

His ability to love had died with his mother.

CHAPTER ONE

Boston, June 21, 2019

"Do you think it's a boy or a girl?" Mia's friend Carla asked, taking a sip of coffee from a paper cup.

Mia's fingers were warm where they touched the smooth black-and-white ultrasound picture. On it was a little human. The round form of the head, the perfect curve of the vertebrae, the five little fingers waving at her filled her heart with so much love, it was about to explode.

The smells assaulting her in the Massachusetts General Hospital cafeteria made Mia slightly nauseated. Coffee, for which she could kill; donuts; and a hint of bleach. Doctors and nurses in uniforms sat together having lunch, visitors hunkered down at separate tables—some chatting with friends and family, others staring tiredly into the distance. A couple of yuccas stood in the corners by the floor-to-ceiling windows. The cafeteria buzzed quietly with voices.

"I don't know." Mia touched the little hand on the ultrasound with her thumb and smiled. It was a boy. Somehow, she just knew. She didn't want to share the knowledge with anyone, as though it was an intimate secret between her and the baby.

Carla and Mia sat near the window. At the table behind Carla was an old lady in a salad-green suit. Her hair as white as snow, a cup of tea on the table, she was knitting, the needles in her hands jumping up and down like the lines of a vitals monitor. The lady stole a curious glance at Mia and the ultrasound picture in her hand. Mia's breath caught in her throat. How strange. Mia flashed a polite smile at the lady.

"A mafia boss's baby... Still can't believe it." Carla shook her head, then leaned closer and dropped her voice to a whisper. "I thought you wanted to break up with him."

Cold sweat ran down Mia's spine at the mention of her ex-boyfriend. "I left him."

"You did? When? Why didn't you tell me?"

"Three days ago. Three of the happiest days of my life."

Carla's eyes lay on the ultrasound. "But he doesn't know about the baby, does he?"

"No. Of course not."

"What would happen if he found out?"

Mia's stomach dropped. "He'd never let me go. You didn't tell your brother you saw me here, did you?" Mia glanced around. "I must be paranoid, but I still keep looking over my shoulder. I can't really believe Dan agreed it was over."

Carla laughed nervously. "I can't believe I introduced you two in the first place! To think, if it wasn't for him, you'd be a pediatrician now. We'd work here together."

Mia shuddered, and the sleeve of her long summer dress shifted enough to reveal the yellowing bruise on her forearm. She blushed and moved to cover it, but Carla noticed. Her eyes darted away, as if she had just seen something too private. Mia's cheeks burned.

"That's all right." Mia pursed her lips. "I'll never let a man treat me like that again. Tomorrow I'm starting a new life. No men. Just me and the baby. Away from Boston."

Carla frowned. "Are you leaving?"

"I got a job far from here, in the middle of nowhere. I can't finish my residency program yet, but someday I will. My new life starts tomorrow morning when I get on the plane."

Carla's eyebrows rose. "And you are telling me *now*?"

"I couldn't risk it."

As the words left her mouth, a shadow fell over the table, a tall figure silhouetted against the sun. His scent reached Mia's nostrils: elegant masculine cologne and the faintest acrid whiff of gun oil. Painful shivers ran across her whole body, and she moved her hand to hide the ultrasound under the table, but his heavy palm smacked the picture to the tabletop. His dry, warm skin burned her icy cold hand.

"Couldn't risk what?" His voice purred next to her ear, his breath stinging her cheek.

He released her hand and pulled on the ultrasound, but she clenched it so tight her fingernails whitened. He jerked it from her hand, cutting her finger. Blood smeared the edge of the image.

Mia jumped up, kicking her chair back, and all eyes shot to her. Her pulse beat in her temples, her chest hurt, and her legs turned to jelly. Outside, Dan's bodyguards, Romeo and Carl, stood waiting. Her stomach dropped.

Dan's eyes were intense as he took in every detail of the ultrasound. He was a handsome man, with short dark hair and large dark eyes with long and thick lashes. He had high cheekbones, and his square jaw was clean shaven. He wore one of his tailored charcoal Italian suits with a white shirt and no tie. He looked like a CEO or a law firm partner—the illusion that Mia had fallen for three years earlier, when they'd first met. She should have suspected something, silly her. No CEO or lawyer had the mountain of pure muscle Dan had acquired from daily combat training. The mistake had cost her everything.

He met her gaze, and a chill washed over her. "I can't believe. That you hid this. From me." His voice was like the distant roar of a truck.

Mia began shaking. "How did you find me?"

"Little bird told me you went to an ob-gyn, and I wanted to make sure you were all right." He glanced at Carla.

Shock hit Mia like a train. "How could you, Carla?"

Carla looked away. "I'm so sorry, Mia! I had no idea you two split up! And I didn't tell *him*."

"You told Gabe?"

Carla nodded. Gabe was Carla's brother who worked for Dan.

Nausea rose in Mia's stomach again. She shouldn't think about it. Not now. She needed to deal with Dan. She took a cleansing breath, like every time she had dealt with his crazy temper. More collected, she met his dark gaze.

"We are over, remember?"

He laughed, then his face turned into an emotionless mask. "Not after this. You are carrying my child. Do you think I'm going to let it grow up in a broken home?"

"There is no home for him with you—"

"Him?" An emotion touched his eyes. "A boy?"

She cursed herself. Dan had always dreamed of having a son. "I'm not sure."

"But you think it's a boy."

"I don't know, Dan! What does it matter?"

"You're right. It doesn't. A boy or a girl, I won't let my child grow up with separated parents. This changes everything. You come back to me, we get married, and we work on our relationship. We'll go to a shrink."

Mia's lips trembled. "But you don't love me, Dan."

His eyes turned black. "You are wrong. I never stopped loving you, *bella*."

The words every woman craved to hear turned Mia's blood into ice. She shook her head. "We're over. No amount of counseling can fix us. Too much has happened. The women, your temper..."

She only needed to get him to let her go home. Hell, just let her go, period. She'd disappear.

"You're right, but you are making me a better man. I'm more in control since you have been in my life than ever before. I'll work on my temper, and there will be no more women. I'll make you see the man you once loved."

That was impossible. She *had* loved him until she'd learned the truth about his occupation—something he hadn't revealed until they'd moved in together. She raised her chin. "How will you make me feel anything for you? Will you beat me again?"

His nostrils flared, and the vein on his temple twitched. "Don't. If you want me to work on my temper, I'll work on my temper. I won't touch a hair on your head. Not like *that*." Then he added in a low voice, "I hated when I did that to you."

How many times had she heard that over the past two and a half years?

"I am *not* coming back."

He grabbed her hand and pulled her to his chest. "Yes, you are."

She struggled to free herself, useless of course. But making a scene could be her chance.

"Let me go or I'll scream," Mia spat.

"No, you won't, bella." Dan moved his arm, and through the thin silk of her dress, she felt the cold barrel of his gun.

Needles pricked her from head to toe. "You won't shoot the mother of your child!"

"I will if she brings the cops down on me."

Mia's gut twisted, her free hand shot to her belly and lay on it protectively. She scanned the cafeteria for help. People glanced at them with curiosity, probably assuming a troubled couple argued. Carla only looked into her cup like a naughty puppy. That old lady in the green suit stopped knitting and watched Mia with concern. But what could a grandma do against Dan and his two bodyguards?

"Help," Mia mouthed to her.

But the woman didn't even twitch.

Dan picked up Mia's purse, shoved it to her, then dragged Mia after him, towards the doors for cafeteria staff. They walked past a bathroom door that read Employees Only and carried on towards the emergency exit. Desperation burned Mia like a fever. She had been so close to escaping Dan, to giving her baby a better future, a normal life—not a life inside the mafia.

But she'd failed. Dan now had a reason to find her anywhere she went. He had connections, ways of locating her, of chaining her to him. She'd had a chance after he had finally agreed to end the toxic relationship that had eaten her up physically and emotionally.

But she'd blown it. She never should have met with Carla. If she'd only waited until tomorrow...

They'd turned the corner of the empty corridor when a voice echoed behind them.

"Wait!"

They stopped and turned around, hope making Mia dizzy. But it was only the old lady.

"What?" Dan barked.

She stopped in front of them, small and harmless, not a trace of fear in her eyes.

"Listen, sweetheart." She talked directly to Mia with an accent that resembled German. "I have a way for you to escape, but it is not an easy path. There is a man who needs you, and you need him—a Viking."

Dan chuckled. "What, a Minnesota Viking? What are you blabbering about?"

"Expect strange things." She did not stop looking at Mia. "You will not believe them to be possible, but they will be the truth."

Mia swallowed. She had no idea what the lady was talking about, but Dan's grip around her arm became stronger and began hurting her, and she started to worry about the woman's safety. "You need to go. Now," Mia said.

"Honey, you forgot something back at the table." The woman's hand went into her purse, and Dan pointed his gun at her. But the woman removed a golden object. Mia squinted. Something like a spindle, from fairy tales?

What a random thing. The old lady held out the spindle. "Take it, you forgot it."

This was crazy. An escape? A golden spindle? A Viking that needed her?

Dan's hand had already stretched out to the spindle.

But there was something so deadly serious in the old lady's face, and so much strength in her gaze, as if destiny itself looked into Mia's eyes. She slapped away Dan's arm and reached out to the spindle. The lady's eyes smiled at that.

What did Mia logically expect would happen? Nothing. Maybe the lady would tase Dan, or maybe she had pepper spray, or maybe she was a retired karate world champion.

Or maybe it was a mean joke.

In any case, Mia went with it. Once the spindle touched her hand, a buzzing vibration went through her, and her head spun for real. Nausea made her stomach heave. The world around her began evaporating. The last thing she saw was Dan's astonished face, his hands grabbing at thin air in the place where she had stood a moment ago, and joy filled her nonexistent body.

And then everything disappeared.

CHAPTER TWO

Lomdalen, Norway, June 21, 875 AD

Hakon flung open the door from his bedchamber to the mead hall, and the scent of a feast cooking hit him in the face. The two hearths running along the center of the mead hall both had rows of cauldrons. Women were cutting meat, chopping vegetables, and kneading dough on the tables around the hearths.

It was the day of the solstice. Finally, the long wait for the pieces of his plan to fall together was over, and Hakon blazed inside.

"I said a supper, not a feast!" he roared at the cooks.

The women looked up at him, eyes wide. A child shrieked.

"Go on, people." Solveig separated from the row of women.

One of her legs was bad, and she wobbled towards him while wiping her hands on her apron. She was the healer of the village, and the midwife to his mother when he had been born. She studied his face. Her eyes stopped on the birthmark in the form of a snarling wolf's head that surrounded his left eye and then spread across his temple and cheekbone and up to his hairline.

"Solveig!" he said. "Do you not need to attend to my wounded men?"

The first raids of the season had not gone well without Hakon, who had stayed home because he did not want to miss the summer solstice.

"Come, Hakon." She stopped in front of him. "The people get a new mistress today. They want a wedding."

"*They* want a wedding?"

She was small, but she was the only person in the whole village who did not shake from fear when he talked to her.

"Clearly, you do not," she said.

"That is right, I do not. No happy wedding to *his* daughter is possible. There is nothing to celebrate."

Solveig crossed her arms over her chest. "Maybe there is. Maybe she will be good for you."

"There is no one in all nine worlds on Yggdrasil who would be good for me," Hakon snarled.

Solveig cocked her head. Hakon hated when she had that look. As if he were a little boy who had been naughty and tried to hide it.

"Do it for the people then, Jarl. Give them hope. The hope of a normal life."

Hakon breathed out a deep sigh and held her gaze. "There is no hope for them, Solveig. Not while I'm their jarl. You know that."

She shook her head. "I wish you would stop with your nonsense. No hope?" She scoffed. "You wait and see. Maybe this woman is exactly the hope you need."

"The only hope I need is for her father to stay alive so that *I* can kill him."

He walked past her towards the gates of the mead hall. "Stop the cooking!" he thundered without looking at anyone. "Preserve the food. There will be no wedding feast."

Disappointed sighs ran through the mead hall. As he approached the exit, people passed by him carrying firewood, and buckets with water. Children carried vegetables. As always, their eyes darted away from him. A girl passing by with a basket full of parsnips up to her chin—Hakon remembered her name was Ledis—could not turn her eyes away from him and stumbled upon the threshold. Parsnips flew, and she was about to meet the floor face-first.

Hakon darted towards her and caught her under her armpits before she fell. Parsnips thumped gently against the floor around them. The girl's eyes widened, she snatched her arms from his grip and ran away with a squeal.

"Does the child think I'll eat her?" Hakon growled.

Solveig wobbled to him and began picking up parsnips. "Maybe. Mothers scare children with stories of you so that they will not walk outside in the dark. The wedding would help make them see a different side of you."

"They have known me their whole lives."

"And they have been afraid of you just as long."

His jaw clenched, Hakon walked outside, anger and frustration seething inside of him like the deep waters in Helheim. He was about to invite another person into his life who would be just as terrified.

Hakon approached his new horse. It stood by the entrance, and it neighed and jerked its head as he came near, its eyes bulging, afraid of the smell of his wolf-hide cloak.

"Easy, Wind, easy," Hakon said, petting the horse's neck. "The cloak is already sixteen winters old, the wolf long dead."

Hakon mounted Wind and guided him through the village,

moving toward the forest. People resumed talking behind him, as if a threat had suddenly been lifted.

His *Hersir*, Torfi, had suggested going with him in case of an ambush, but Hakon was sure there would not be any. If Nyr had wanted to kill him, he would have done it back in autumn when Hakon was at his mercy.

He passed by the dark, weathered longhouses he had seen his whole life, the barn, the fish drying racks, the pit for smoking. The village swarmed with activity—people were preparing to meet their new mistress, the one who would end the danger coming from King Nyr.

Roofs had holes, gables were worn by weather, sheds, lean-tos and fences slanted. The streets should have been boarded. The dirt would turn into slush once it rained. The village was alive with the sounds of its everyday activities: the *tong-tong* of the blacksmith's hammer, the mooing and squawking, the talking and occasional squeals of playing children. The air was filled with woodsmoke and the scents of cooked meat and baked bread, in order to welcome princess Arinborg.

There was something else, barely noticeable. A shift in the air, as if destiny was cooking something. Hakon hoped the Norns were weaving him the same destiny he had been breathing ever since his father had died two years ago.

The death of his enemy.

After a short while of climbing up the low slope of the mountain through the woods, he reached the sacred grove. Despite himself, curiosity stirred his stomach. He hoped Arinborg would be cursed by some sort of mark, as well, or was simply ugly. Then it would be easier to keep his distance from her. If she found out about his plan to kill her father, she could warn him.

The rocks of the sacred grove between the trees blackened. It was a large round clearing, with pines, aspens, and birches surrounding it like walls. Rocks rose like the shoulders of a giant between the trees, seeming as if they would move if you blinked. Right in the middle was a rune stone, next to the altar rock where ritual blots, the sacrifices, were made.

And next to that, a woman.

Hakon's heart jumped and froze for a moment, taking her in.

She was leaning with both her hands against the rune stone, panting. Her long, strawberry-blonde hair shielded her face in waves. She was dressed in a beautiful, rich dress the likes of which he had never seen. The cloth looked thin, flowing, like water, down her body. Giant flowers the colors of spring decorated it, and it made her look like the spirit of nature awakening, a creature out of this world. Over her shoulder was a violet leather purse.

Hakon cursed under his breath. Why did Arinborg need to be so fair?

Before Hakon could greet her, a bear appeared from between the trees behind Arinborg. He growled and stood up. Across the clearing, to Hakon's left, bees buzzed. Last year, Solveig had noticed a beehive in a tree, and no one had touched it on account of it being blessed by the gods.

Hakon's blood chilled. The bear wanted the honey, but it likely thought Arinborg wanted it, too.

The bear roared, and Arinborg's head lifted to look at the animal. She was beautiful: big eyes, soft mouth, high cheekbones. Hakon's stomach twisted in fear for her. The bear launched itself forward, and so did Hakon on the horse.

Arinborg looked up at him, her eyes wide, and Hakon leaned to one side and grabbed her as Wind passed by her. He put her over the horse in front of him.

The bear charged them, rising on its hind legs and slashing the air next to the horse's side as Wind galloped past. Hakon turned Wind around, and they rode right past the rune stone and away from the sacred grove.

Wind galloped down the path a bit too quickly for his liking, and Arinborg began struggling, then yelled, "What's going on, you barbarian? Let me go!"

The female sounded willful, no better than her father. And if she was like her father, he would never feel anything for her besides hatred.

He glanced back but did not see the bear anywhere around the trees, and the footworn path behind him was empty. Hakon pulled the reins a little to slow the horse.

"This barbarian saved you from a bear, Princess." Hakon held her still in front of him, her body warming his skin through the silk of her dress. She continued struggling.

"Stop the horse!"

"I can if you want the bear to catch up. But let me suggest it is better we are as far away from it as possible. If you continue to struggle, you will fall and break you neck. Is that something you want?"

She kept silent. Soon they arrived at the village, and people stopped and watched them, wide-eyed. Of course. The Beast brought his future wife home thrown over the back of his horse like a sack of wheat.

Hakon stopped Wind by the mead hall and dismounted, then put his hands around Arinborg's hips to help her down. The gesture was probably improper, but he did not care. The curves of her hips were nicely rounded beneath the thin cloth under his fingers. Her body was both soft and firm, and warm, oh so warm. Her skin slid under the material as if it were silk, as well.

Arinborg landed on the ground and turned to face him, standing between the horse and Hakon. Her scent tickled his nostrils, so sweet and clean. She smelled like spring flowers and something else...some indefinable spice that seemed to belong to her alone.

Her big green eyes were a little slanted. How could she have such thick eyelashes? He was drowning in her eyes. Her cheeks were flushed, the color of a young dog-rose bloom. Her lips, full and soft, were slightly parted. The urge to kiss her, to taste her tongue, to take her mouth and bite her full lip rose in his body like a storm, his heart drumming in his ears.

No. He could not. He had decided he would not be involved with her. Not with his heart.

But he wanted her. The feel of her legs under his fingers, her scent, her beauty. He could not resist her, even though he needed to. She was his bride. He could have her if he wanted to...

And oh, Loki, he wanted to.

"Let all the gods be damned." He leaned towards her to claim the kiss.

But as he did, her eyes widened even more in surprise, she doubled up and vomited. Warm liquid soaked through his tunic on his chest. He closed his eyes, his jaw tightening, as the people around them giggled, and his bride wiped her mouth with the back of her hand, studying him from under her lashes.

Of course. She must have been disgusted by his mark so much, she could not stop her feelings. Anger seethed in him.

Arinborg looked around them, and her hand shot to her throat. "Where am I?"

"In Lomdalen, of course," Hakon said and took a step back. He needed to clean his tunic.

"Where is that?" her voice trailed off to a whisper.

He squinted at her. "What are you talking about, Princess? You know where it is. You traveled here yourself."

Arinborg swallowed, her hands were looking for something behind her.

And then she turned and ran. Her skirts flapped on the wind, her long, graceful legs flashing. Shock froze him in place.

Was he that ugly? So ugly she had to run from him, breaking her father's oath?

Hakon looked at his people to see if anyone understood what had just happened, but everyone had the same stunned look.

Then Hakon came to his senses and ran after her. She had to marry him. It was done. Agreed. Everything depended on it.

He reached her after two longhouses; she was not the best of runners. Grabbing her upper arm, he turned her to himself. She was breathing hard, but still tried to kick him.

"Get off me!"

He pressed her to his chest so that she would stop struggling. "Princess, you must honor your father's agreement and marry me. If you wanted to change your mind, you should have done it earlier. It is too late now."

"I don't know what you're talking about. What is this, a movie set? A reality show? Where are the cameras? Let me go."

She kicked his ankle, and pain shot through him. He tightened his grip.

"Why are you speaking these strange words?"

Then doubt hit him like a cold wave of the North Sea, and he shook her slightly. "You are Arinborg, aren't you?"

Her face straightened. She froze, watching him carefully. "What would happen if I wasn't?"

"If you are not Arinborg, you are an imposter who is pretending to be a princess and trying to marry a jarl. You would be judged and killed."

She paled, and her chest rose and fell, making him painfully aware of her soft breasts brushing against him, stirring desire in him like liquid fire. "Are you Arinborg or not?"

She pressed out a strained smile, one hand covering her

stomach. He hoped she was not going to vomit a second time.

"Of course I am. I was testing you."

She forced her face to relax—he saw the effort. But beneath the mask, that same frightened tension showed, that frown of someone who was terrified.

The expression he had seen around him his whole life.

"Good," he said, releasing her but still holding her elbow. "Look. I do not want this marriage any more than you do. But it is settled between your father and me. I am not Brandr, god of beauty, but you will marry me. And if you do not like me, what bad luck for you."

Arinborg's eyebrows rose in surprise, but Hakon continued. "We are bound now, whether you find me handsome or not. You will be my wife. It is done."

Even though she did not say anything, a cold resolve turned the spring-grass green in those beautiful eyes into malachite stone at his words. She tensed her jaw, seeming to withdraw somewhere deep inside herself.

"Fine," she spat through her teeth.

"Let us go." Hakon jerked and dragged her, hating that he was forcing an unwilling woman to marry him, and hating that she awoke in him a tiny part that wished she was not scared of the Beast like everyone else. That she would marry him gladly.

He shut that part down.

CHAPTER THREE

The mouthwatering aroma of stew steamed from a clay bowl in front of Mia. She sat alone at a long table, her whole body tense, her shoulders aching.

She looked around the room. Women cooked food on open fires, throwing prying glances at her. Hakon talked to a plump woman so short she only reached the middle of his chest, who looked up at him as if he were as tall as an electric pole.

There was no electricity here, she realized. The dark house had no windows; the only light came from the oil lamps chain-hung from the beams. The building was wooden and crude, so was the furniture. Most people were blond. Women wore long, square woolen dresses. Men wore tunics and trousers tucked into stockings at the knee.

Where was she, and how did she get here?

She had been in Mass Gen. Dan had dragged her away, and that lady had come to her rescue. Then Mia had touched the golden spindle, and her body had disappeared right next to Dan.

And then she had opened her eyes in a clearing in the

woods, and a bear had roared, and then a huge man on a horse, with an ax and a sword, had grabbed her—Hakon, she now knew.

The strangeness of this place terrified her. The fact that she spoke a foreign language she'd never learned terrified her. Hakon terrified her—the sight of him, giant, powerful, intimidating, and that birthmark that made him look as if one side of him was dark and the other light. As if two creatures lived in him. One man, the other beast.

And the second reminded her of Dan.

She needed to get out of here, but she had to figure out how first. She rejoiced at the chance to be left alone, to try to understand what had happened to her.

She lay a hand on her still-flat belly. "We're okay," she whispered. "We'll survive."

Her stomach growled. How could she be hungry after vomiting? But she was, and she scooped up a bit of stew with the wooden spoon and brought it to her mouth. She closed her eyes in sheer bliss as she savored the rich taste.

The woman with the golden spindle had said something about—

Viking.

Mia choked, spraying a mouthful of stew across the table as she jumped up. Everyone looked at her in astonishment.

"Is the food not to your liking, Princess?" Hakon asked.

"Are you a Viking?" she gasped out.

Hakon frowned. "I did not go Viking this year yet. I did not want to miss meeting you."

"*Go* Viking?"

His frown deepened, danger written all over his face. Crossing the room towards her in a few quick strides, he stood right in front of her, and all the air was sucked out of her lungs.

He spoke in that husky, low voice of his, and it sent hot

shivers through her skin. "Going Viking. Raiding. Pirating. Are you testing me again? Asking your pointless questions, as if you hear things for the first time." He grabbed her arm and pulled her to his chest—it felt like hitting a warm brick wall. "Is it my patience that you are testing? Because I don't have a lot of it. Go on a little, and you'll find out."

His face was so close to hers, she could see the green in his pale golden eyes. They were magnetic, the eyes of a conqueror, someone who would not stop until he got what he wanted.

Dan looked at her like that.

Memories came rushing through her. Pain, helplessness, fear closed her lungs and choked her throat.

No!

She had just escaped Dan, and she would not let another man do to her what he had done: abuse her body, take away her freedom, and break her spirit.

Threaten her baby.

She jerked her arm from his grip and shoved him away. Startled, he swayed back, face alarmed.

"I already told you to get off me!" she yelled, and headed towards the exit in broad strides.

She'd be damned if she stayed one more minute with a man like Dan. What was Hakon's deal? She didn't want to know. All she wanted, was to take her baby to safety.

She stepped outside, and fresh, sweet air filled her lungs. All around the village, mountains shot like walls into the sky, and at the other end of the village, a giant, still inlet of water curved between them. Ships were docked by the shore—long wooden ships with high curved bows and round shields along the sides. Cows and sheep grazed, chickens squawked. One house down, a blacksmith hammered at a giant anvil.

Mia shuddered and looked down at her stomach. "Where

are we, peanut?" she whispered, still not able to believe what her senses were showing her.

"You will not escape," Hakon said next to her, and a mixture of fear and excitement ran over her skin like a shower of sparks. "And if you want me to stop touching you, you need to stop behaving as if Loki took your mind."

He was like a mountain made of human flesh. He did not grab her or shove her or move a finger towards her this time, but his body heat touched her gently.

Tall and muscular, he moved with a predatory grace, every action efficient, economical. Even though Dan was also tall, he was still much shorter than Hakon, much less muscular, too. Where Dan was sophistication and style with his tailored Italian suit and perfect haircut, Hakon was simplicity and roughness. It was like comparing an aristocrat to a barbarian.

Hakon's gaze pinned her to the ground. Might and a power of will seeped through him. His scent...god, his scent. Hay, leather, and sea. And his voice...deep, melodic, sexy, the perfect voice to read erotic audiobooks.

The pinkish-brown birthmark around his eye made him unforgettable, mysterious, like a dark superhero who hadn't decided if he was fighting for good or evil. Did he feel self-conscious about it? Most people probably would. But Hakon radiated anger, like an invisible force field around him.

"Do you not want to marry me?" His voice rung like steel. Did she hear an edge of vulnerability in it? He looked pointedly in front of him, his profile stern.

What would Princess Arinborg say to that?

"That is not for me to decide," she said.

She and Arinborg must have that in common, she thought.

"Let me suggest that you follow your own wisdom. The decision was made for you. All you need to do is obey."

Arinborg might have done just that, but Mia wouldn't. She

looked around. How could she escape? Hakon watched her like a hawk. Maybe when he was asleep or busy with something else… She glanced at the forest visible behind the roofs. Somewhere there, was the path they had followed when she arrived.

If she had traveled back in time—and oh, how ridiculous it sounded—maybe returning to the clearing where Hakon had found her would help her find some way back to Boston. She had been touching the rock when she arrived, its surface sending a strange buzzing sensation over her body, her fingers almost sinking into the stone. If she touched it again, would she return to her own time?

There were two problems with going back to the grove. One, the bear could still be there. Two, Dan could be waiting for her on the other side.

Yes, the old lady had helped her escape. But was her solution better than being under Dan's control? If she got back, Dan would find out. If she lived on the same planet, he'd find her. He had a vast network of mafia connections, but sometimes she felt as if she lived in a sci-fi movie and he'd implanted a chip in her body. He always knew where she was.

Technically, being here with these Vikings would be the best place to hide from Dan.

But no. She was pregnant. Mia put her hand on her lower belly. *Are you all right, peanut? Did all this time traveling hurt you?* Mia focused inward, trying to feel a life inside of her, although as a doctor she was aware that there was no way she could really know. But a little needle pricked in her lower belly again like it had during the whole first trimester.

Yes, he was fine. She knew it.

Now that she was a little over three months pregnant and in her second trimester, the chances of something going wrong were much smaller. She also felt better now: no nausea, no tiredness. But there was another thing to consider. She could not possibly give birth here. Childbirth without modern medicine was dangerous, and the threats to health were enormous. Not to mention the unsanitary conditions.

First, she needed to get back to Boston. Then, she'd find a way to escape Dan.

So she would continue to be Princess Arinborg until tonight. Anything to save her baby. When Hakon fell asleep, she'd sneak out and get back to that clearing.

"You're right," Mia said. "I'll follow my wisdom." Her voice jumped and betrayed her.

Hakon glanced at her. "Good. Finally." But he frowned as he said it.

She would follow her wisdom. The wisdom of not letting another man rule her life, no matter how powerful he was...or attractive.

CHAPTER FOUR

Mia listened to the night. The house was silent beyond the door of Hakon's bedchamber, and the man himself wheezed peacefully on the floor by the bed. Mia rose on one elbow on the mattress, fur blanket sliding down her arms. Even though a female servant had brought her a night shift, Mia had refused to change into anything before going to bed, so she was fully dressed.

Hakon had informed her that she would sleep in his bedroom, the only room besides the huge main hall. Usually guests stayed in the sleeping alcoves in the giant hall, as far as Mia understood. But he had assured her he had no intention of touching her before they were married. And even though she had said she would listen to her own wisdom earlier, she knew he did not fully trust her.

She needed to take this chance to escape. Heart thumping, she let out a long, quiet breath, threw the blanket off and stepped onto the wooden floor. She found her sandals and put them on, careful not to make a sound. Despite her soft steps, one plank of the floor creaked slightly.

Mia froze. Hakon stirred and turned onto his side. Mia swallowed. She took her purse and put it over her shoulder like a messenger bag.

Her pulse drummed in her ears. She unclenched her hands and shook them to relieve the tension. "We'll be okay, peanut," she mouthed and patted her belly.

Then she continued across the room, cold sweat streaming down her back as she passed right by Hakon's head. He slept on a sheepskin, so handsome, his face calm, relaxed. She had not seen him like that when he was awake. She wondered what it would be like to be his wife, his strong arms wrapped around her as they slept.

Silly.

By some miracle, she made it to the door without waking him up. She cracked it open a little and peered out, but nobody was up and moving around.

Mia slowly opened the door. Her pulse raced, as if she had just run a marathon. Sweat dampened her whole body, and her hands shook.

Mia entered the great hall and closed the door behind her. People snored from the corners of the hall, hopefully masking any sounds as she headed for the entrance.

When she reached the double doors, she opened one a little to peek outside. Nearby, a man sat on a stool leaning back against the wall, his chin on his chest. He looked like he was asleep.

So Hakon had left a guard. Mia needed to be careful. She opened the door bit by bit, and it made a low screeching sound. Mia's heart stopped. She froze, her eyes pinned to the guard.

The man stirred, straightened, scratched his face, and looked around. Mia hid behind the door and waited, panting.

After a while, she glanced at the guard. He had nodded off again.

On heavy legs, she slid through the opening. Outside, the night was chilly, and her skin was soon covered with goose bumps. The dry ground muffled her steps. The guard continued to wheeze, and Mia glanced around to make sure no one noticed her.

But the only movement was the wind rustling through the trees around the village. Her chest heaving with hope, she rushed towards the forest and the path that led up the hill to the clearing and the strange rock with the runes.

Hakon looked at his empty bed in the darkness.

Something had awoken him a moment ago, an instinct to check if his bride was all right. But she had disappeared. He sat up. Had she gone out to relieve herself?

No. He knew in his gut that she had run away again.

A low growl escaped his throat.

"Wake uuuup!" he roared as he flew into the mead hall, the door slamming behind him.

Men and women stumbled wearily from their sleeping alcoves.

"Search for the princess!" he shouted.

He ran towards the entrance, looking for her. How could he have trusted her word? He had sensed something was amiss, her reluctance, her odd behavior.

She had fooled him.

No, he had fooled himself by letting his guard down. She had told him she would accept her fate, and he had believed her. Oaf. He had wanted to believe her because a tiny part of him wanted her to be his wife, even though his curse clearly terrified her.

He should not have taken his eyes off her for a moment. He should not have fallen asleep. He should have put more guards at the entrance.

She had chosen to escape him—to escape the curse. Too bad, he thought, clenching his teeth. The curse was coming for her.

As he walked outside, Loker, who he had put on guard duty, looked around with the bewilderment of someone who had just woken up.

"Thor strike you with his hammer, you were *asleep!*" Hakon roared.

"Jarl—"

"Go wake up the men. And you better hope we catch her before she gets too far."

Loker paled and rushed towards the next house.

Hakon put his hands around his mouth. "Wake uuup!" he thundered.

Soon, his men scattered on the streets of the village, their faces concerned, their ax blades glistening in the moonlight. "Take horses, take hounds. Princess Arinborg ran away. Find her. Look in the woods, on the water, under tree stumps, in caves. If she disappears or comes to harm, we invite an angry enemy to our doorstep."

His men nodded, their faces stern. They split into groups and went in all directions.

Hakon took Wind and straddled his back. He looked around. The princess could be anywhere. But something—instinct or destiny—made him look at the footworn path into the woods. She could have headed home, and the easiest way would have been by water if she had wanted to hide the traces.

She could take one of the small fishing boats; a woman could easily row one.

And yet Hakon wanted to take the same path that had brought him to her in the first place.

He led Wind there.

Two men accompanied him. The way through the dark woods was slow, and Hakon's gut knotted. He could not let her slip through his fingers. And if the bear was still there...or wolves?

His heart chilled at the thought that Arinborg could face the same fate as his mother.

Why had she escaped? She could not stand him. The pain of being unwanted, rejected squeezed his core like a fist made of ice. He felt like a dirty dog nobody wanted. The thought of being his wife, spending her life with him, sharing his bed must have been so repulsive to her that she decided to break her father's word.

She had slid out alone into the woods. Or maybe she had help. Maybe she had another man.

Even though he had just met her, the thought of her with another made his blood seethe like hot oil. He would not tolerate a betrayal.

And then he saw her.

The white of her dress flashing between black trees, its pattern of spring flowers now dark at night. It was not possible to run up the hill, but she walked as fast as she could.

And further to the left, he saw the opening to the sacred grove. It was clearly her destination.

Why?

Did someone wait for her?

Was she supposed to give a message to Nyr's spy? Had she found out something about Hakon's plan?

His teeth clenched. Gods, he would not let this happen.

"Ha!" he hurried Wind, and Arinborg glanced back, startled.

She sped up, heading towards the center of the grove, her arms stretched out in front of her as if she wanted to grab something.

Hakon reached the clearing, but he could not see anyone besides his bride, just the rock. Did someone hide behind it?

He stopped Wind, jumped down, and ran after her, ax in his hand in case someone appeared.

"Arinbooorg!" he called.

He was catching up with her, but she was almost at the rock. He pressed on, and just before she could touch it, he grabbed her by the waist with one arm and they both rolled on the ground. He lay on top of her, pinning her down, her face astonished, then furious. She hit his chest with both hands.

"Let me go!" she yelled, her cheeks flushed, her forehead glistening from sweat. He became aware of her soft, warm body under him, her squished breasts against him, her legs that warmed him. He imagined her wanting him. He imagined that she sweated not from running from him, but from not getting enough of him. He imagined her long legs spreading for him, hugging his waist, urging him inside of her.

But these were dreams.

Her face tensed. Desperate. Disgusted.

"No, you will not escape," he growled. Her expression stabbed him, and he pushed down the pain. He glanced at his men. "Check the grounds. There's someone she must have wanted to meet."

His men galloped around the clearing and rode into the woods.

When he looked back at her face, he could not breathe. She was so beautiful. Her cheeks flushed, her lips like rubies, her hair like honey. Her eyes...it pained him to look at her eyes, they were so pretty. And so full of fear and anger.

"Who were you meeting? What did you want to tell them?"

Tears streamed down her face.

"No one. I wanted to run away from *you*." She spat the words into his face like poison.

He had never felt so unwanted, so ugly. So much like a beast.

"You leave me no choice. You are a prisoner now. We will marry as soon as we get back to the village. And you will be under guard until you accept your life here. And if you are afraid that I will touch you as a man touches his wife, if it is my ugliness that bothers you, I give you my word, I will not claim you in that way until you ask me yourself."

He stood and helped her up.

"They might call me a beast, but I am not *that* kind of beast."

He did not look at her as he said that, dragging her towards Wind. But out of the corner of his eye, he thought he saw her face soften.

CHAPTER FIVE

He'd caught her, this Viking, this mammoth. Was she destined to get caught by men? Back in Boston, and now here, in what she had come to believe must be Viking Scandinavia.

Mia's back was pressed against Hakon's front as they rode, his body warming her, his strong arms on both sides of her, holding the reins. She breathed heavily, feeling as if there was not enough air in his presence, her cheeks burning like hot coals.

She was still afraid of him. She would have been an idiot not to be—he could snap her in half with his bare arms if he wanted to.

But he also affected her in ways Dan never had, making her knees weak and her skin damp. And when he'd told her he wouldn't touch her, a tension somewhere deep in her gut had released. Part of Mia believed him, even though she had heard similar promises from Dan countless times.

Another part screamed that she would be insane to trust Hakon's word just like that. She could be wrong. God knew, she had been *so* wrong about Dan. But she believed she'd learned her lesson.

As they rode into Lomdalen, the sky behind the dark mountains glowed pink. The air was crisp and lush with the scent of dew and grass.

"How did you find me?" Mia asked.

Hakon didn't answer for a while. When he spoke, his ribcage vibrated against her back, and Mia suppressed an impulse to lean against him and close her eyes. "It was too quiet. I awoke, and you were gone."

"But how did you know where I would be?"

"I did not, Arinborg. I have this instinct. Like an animal. Something told me to follow you through the woods. But even if I had been wrong, I would have found you. My men are looking for you everywhere now."

Mia bit her lip. She could not escape him, just like she could not escape Dan.

He stopped the horse next to Solveig's house, which was three buildings down from the great house. He jumped to the ground and stood there, waiting, looking up at her. He was so tall his eyes were on the same level as her waist. He offered his hand and raised his eyebrows.

Hakon was gorgeous in his rough handsomeness. His shoulder-length dark-blond hair framed his face. His beautiful eyes were now almost brown in the light of the dawn. They were set deeper than what might be considered classically handsome. But it made him look unforgettable. Manly. The stubble covering his chin blended from dark blond to ginger to amber. A few scars disturbed his skin, three long and broad ones on his right cheekbone might have been left by the claws of an animal.

"Come down," he said.

"Where are we going?"

"To wed."

Not that again. Being his wife... Mia shivered from the thought of going somewhere alone with him. But whether it was fear or excitement, she couldn't tell.

"You were serious? Now?" Her mouth was as dry as an autumn leaf. Why did marrying a woman he had never seen before mean so much to him?

He nodded. "You are not running away from me again."

We'll see about that, Mia thought, but put her hand in his. She'd wait for a better opportunity to run.

His touch sent liquid starlight up her arm. As Mia began sliding down, Hakon hugged her hips, then his head was right in front of her breasts. She could feel his warm breath through the cloth, and her world shifted. When her feet touched the ground, he didn't let her go. Something ran between them as their eyes locked. Those golden-green eyes—they were almost amber now, in the misty light of dawn. An invisible curtain lifted in them, and his face changed. He became younger, just like she had seen him in his sleep, suddenly vulnerable, open. Raw pain hid there. She knew pain, too.

Hakon blinked and withdrew. His arms released her, and the curtain slid back down. The mask of the Beast was firmly in place again. Cold surrounded Mia instead of his warm arms, and she took a step back. She shouldn't linger. She shouldn't look for humanity in him. And she shouldn't allow any empathy between them. This wasn't her time, her place, or her man.

She was an imposter filling Hakon's bride's shoes. And her life and that of her child were forfeit if he found out before she could escape.

Hakon pressed his lips into a thin line. He tied the reins to the fence by the house. Someone walked out.

It was that small woman who wobbled when she walked.

"Solveig!" Hakon called, and the woman turned around.

"Hakon." Then she noticed Mia. "Ah, you found her."

"Yes. And we shall be wed now."

"Now?" Solveig continued walking down the street, and Hakon took Mia's hand, sending a not-unpleasant tingling sensation up her arm, and drew her after himself.

"Yes, now."

"I must see to the injured first," she threw over her shoulder. "Two more babes got sick."

Mia frowned, the instinct of a doctor making her want to ask about their symptoms, but she bit her tongue. She doubted a Viking princess would know much about medicine.

The desire to help, to heal, to fix pulsed in her like another organ that kept her alive. She had pressed it down and ignored it ever since Dan had made her drop out of the pediatric residency program.

The memory of that night would always haunt her.

Dan and she had been having dinner on the balcony of his Marblehead mansion, celebrating her moving in with him. With the sunset view over the ocean and the amazing meal cooked by a Michelin chef he had hired, Mia had thought there was nothing more romantic. The man she loved wanted to lay the world at her feet.

Dan had stretched his tanned hand over the table and taken hers. "I think it's time you quit the residency program, bella," he'd said.

Mia had gaped. "Quit?"

"We live together now. I will provide for you—you know you have everything your heart desires. I don't want you to get a call in the middle of a dinner party with my business associates. And you wouldn't have time for pampering yourself. I want you to feel like a queen. *My* queen."

"But I don't want to quit. I only have two years left in the program, and I love it—"

His eyes darkened, and for the first time in the six months they'd been together, she could see it was from something other than lust.

"You—*love*—it?" Dan's hand tightened until his knuckles whitened, and Mia gasped in pain. "Is there someone I should know about, Mia?"

"What? No! I'm crazy in love with *you*. I just moved in."

His face relaxed, but his eyes were still cold. So cold, the ocean breeze turned from warm to chilly.

"If you're in love with me," he said, "you quit the job. I don't want to share you with anyone. Or anything."

She couldn't believe her ears. "Come on. Don't force me to make this choice."

He launched across the table and grabbed her by the collar of her dress at the scruff of her neck. Champagne glasses flew, shattering on the patio tiles. He kissed her so hard it was a bite. It was a threat. Then he came around the table and hit her. She flew across the balcony, pain exploding in her head and body as she connected with the hard surface. He sank onto his knees next to her and took a fistful of her hair.

"You will quit your job," he panted into her ear. Mia swallowed back her tears. How could a man who had promised her the world be so cruel to her?

She had spent the night wide awake, listening to Dan's even wheezing by her side. In the morning, while he prepared breakfast downstairs, she'd packed her bag. When she appeared in the kitchen, full of resolve to leave him, Dan's eyes fell on her luggage and went deadly. He put down the orange he was halving. But not the knife.

"Bella, you shouldn't be a pediatrician." Dan walked slowly towards her. "You're not that smart. You don't get to be a doctor *and* a mafia boss's girlfriend. It's either one or the other. And I love you too much to let you go."

A mafia boss? He was right, she wasn't that smart. How had she been fooled into thinking he was a legitimate businessman? How many red flags had she willfully ignored?

He stood barefoot and bare chested in white linen pajama pants, his sculpted body gorgeous and as dangerous as the knife in his hand. "Are you really threatening me?" she asked.

He glanced at the knife, chuckled and put it on the cutting board. "I don't think you want to find out, bella. And don't even think about running out on me. I'll find you anywhere in the world."

She had known then that he would never let her go, that she had to bide her time and wait until he grew bored of her. So she had quit the residency program and focused on surviving whatever was to come. Until she had learned about the baby she carried...

Mia shook off the memories, but the feeling of being trapped with someone deadly clung to her.

Solveig stopped in front of a house that looked newer than the others.

"Solveig, if the babes need help, you attend to them first," Hakon said. "But you are marrying us right after."

Solveig sighed and shook her head in disapproval, but it was clear she'd do it.

She'd already entered the building when Mia blurted out, "Wait! I can help."

Hakon and the woman stared at her, clearly surprised. "You can help?" Solveig said. "Are you a healer?"

Mia swallowed and looked at Hakon, expecting him to see this as a threat, to show disapproval, but he only studied her, puzzled.

"Yes," Mia said, her chin high.

People in that building needed a doctor. And with all due respect to Solveig, Mia was the best shot they had.

"A princess and a healer?" Hakon said in disbelief.

"Yes." Mia met his gaze. "And a good one."

"If this is another trick to try to run away, you are a fool. I am coming in and watching you."

Mia shrugged. At least he hadn't forbidden her to do her job. If anything, he looked impressed.

Inside, the house looked like a smaller version of Hakon's giant hall. Sleeping benches ran along the walls, a long hearth stood in the center of the room, there were no windows. There must have been a dozen people lying on the benches, including children. A woman gave a child a cup to drink from.

"What happened to them?" Mia asked.

"Many got wounded at the battle with your father last autumn," Solveig said. "Several men were injured during raids earlier this spring. The winter was rough, and after a visitor came to the village three weeks ago with a cough, children have been getting ill. Hakon gave up his house for the sick."

Mia looked at him in astonishment.

"Having one place for the sick rather than a sick person in every household saves Solveig time," he grumbled.

"Didn't we sleep in your bedroom? I thought you lived in that giant house?"

"Do you mean the mead hall? I did not live there before this autumn. It was my father's. Even after his death, I did not live there."

Mia looked around. She was no historian, but the idea of a hospital seemed strange for Vikings.

"Aren't the wounded usually tended in their households by their wives, mothers, or sisters?"

"They are. But they get better care if Solveig can help them.

It is hard for her to walk through the whole village with her bad leg."

Who was this man? She didn't know him at all. Dan would've never inconvenienced himself to help others.

"Do not look at me as if Loki stole my mind," he said.

Something warmed inside Mia's chest. She smiled. The anticipation of helping people who needed her lifted her spirits.

"I'm not, Hakon." She respected his decision, but she couldn't tell him that. She should remain distant from him—any sign of affection would give him the wrong idea. She looked around and rubbed her hands together, eager to start the work she'd itched to do for two and a half years. "Now, let's see how our patients are."

CHAPTER SIX

Hakon squinted as the darkness of the house enveloped him with the sweet and pungent scent of cooked herbs. On the sleeping benches to the left were his injured warriors. Spread throughout the rest of the house were children. The sound of their desperate coughing made his own chest ache.

Hakon watched as Arinborg leaned over a girl about eight winters old. The child's face was red as she gasped for air, making whooping noises. She sounded as if she was trying to cough out a fly.

"Has it long been an interest of yours, Arinborg?" Hakon said.

"What?" Arinborg took the child's wrist between her thumb and two fingers and stilled, concentrating. Then she pressed her ear against the girl's chest and listened. She helped her to sit up and listened to her back, after which she pressed the back of her hand against the child's forehead.

"Healing," he said.

Her care, the determination on her face reminded him of his mother, and the thought was both sweet and painful. He remembered how his mother had leaned over him like that when he ran a fever as a child. Only Mother and Solveig cared for him. The rest kept away from his curse, just like his father.

Hakon remembered his mother's face, her big green eyes full of love and worry. The gold of her hair shone in the light of the hearth. She hummed him a song to lull him to sleep. Her soft hand pressed gently at the back of his head as she kept him up so that he could drink an herbal remedy.

A sharp ache tightened his chest at the memory. He did not want it to fade away, though painful.

Arinborg did not stop her examination, but her mouth tensed. "Would that be wrong?"

It seemed Arinborg knew what she was doing, as if she had done it many times. Her eyes were focused, her hands were confident and calm, her face was tight with concentration.

"Not wrong." Hakon shifted his weight. "Unusual."

Solveig came to stand next to him and watched Arinborg.

Arinborg moved to another child and listened to his chest. "Because I'm a princess?"

"Yes. And also because someone like your father allowed it."

Arinborg touched the boy's forehead. He doubled up in a frenzy of violent coughing, and Arinborg's brows knit together. "My father can go to hell," Hakon thought he heard her mutter, but he could not say for certain.

Before he could ask, she turned to Solveig and him. "Running nose, low fever, high-pitched 'whoop' between the coughing attacks... I think these two children have whooping cough. It's highly contagious so there will be more children and adults infected."

Solveig's brows rose. "Infe—what?"

Arinborg hugged her waist, as if protecting herself. "I mean, more people getting sick. And whooping cough is dangerous, especially for babies. I don't have antibio—" She cut herself off and swallowed, her chest rising and falling. It was as if she was looking for words. "Special...herbs," she finished, looking at Hakon expectantly.

Hakon struggled to make sense of what she said. It was as if some of the words were foreign even though she spoke them in the Norse language. Maybe she used the speech of healers and of *gothi*. Healing was the domain of gods, magic, and spirits.

"How do you know all this?" he asked.

"I've always wanted to be a doctor. I mean, a healer. I trained. I helped people. Until I was forced to stop." Her voice broke and her shoulders sank. The life seemed to go out of her as she said those words. Hakon's fists clenched. If Nyr had made her feel like this, how else had he treated her?

"I can help them." She gestured at the children.

Solveig glanced up at Hakon. "The princess seems to know what she is doing."

Hakon believed that. He knew skill and passion for a craft when he saw them. His bride was beautiful, kind, strong, and she was skilled at healing. Warmth spread in his chest as if from a hot stone, and the ice around his heart began to melt. The feeling was as sweet as fresh spring water high up in the mountains.

Awe. Something he did not want to feel for the daughter of his enemy.

Arinborg still looked at him as if she wanted him to say something.

"What is it?" he said.

"Well? Will you *allow* me to help them?" she asked.

Should he forbid her that? Fool. Of course he should. She had impressed him so much he had forgotten the most important thing. Marrying her. Not letting her escape again.

To all gods, he needed to forbid her. If she moved freely under the pretense of gathering herbs and roots and such, she could run away again.

And yet, if she wanted to be a healer, if it would give her comfort and satisfaction in Lomdalen, maybe she would not want to run away anymore. She could be useful to his people. Solveig did not have as much strength as before and could use any help she could get.

"Yes, you may heal the sick," he said, and a giant smile spread on her face, beautiful and precious. Seeing her smile for the first time, he wished he could give her something to be joyful about every day. Not that he should care about his enemy's daughter. He only needed her for cover.

"But after we are wed," he said. "My men will still guard you. I do not trust you."

She nodded. "Solveig, you must have herbs and such."

"Yes, Princess, I do."

"We need something that contains salicylic acid. Let me think…they derive it from a plant…*Filipendula ulmaria*."

She sounded like she was casting a spell. Even Solveig regarded Arinborg with confusion. "What did you say, Princess?" she asked.

"It lowers fever."

"I use meadowsweet to lower fever."

"Yes, that's it! Then we need something with beta-carotene, like carrots, to strengthen the mucous membranes. We need garlic and onion to help fight bacteria…I mean, the sickness. We need oats or barley so that their bodies don't lose as many fluids. I think we need a stew. The sick should eat plenty of it and drink lots of fluids."

Solveig watched her.

"We also need to boil water here in the room. Steam and humidity will help to ease the cough."

"Princess," Solveig said, "if you are right, you might be just the blessing of the gods that we needed. The year Hakon was born, the coughing sickness took nine children. Hakon got sick, too, but survived along with others."

Hakon swallowed. Solveig's words made him think of his mother. How she must have been worried, how she must have nursed him, whooping and red-faced just like these children.

"He survived whooping cough as a baby?" Arinborg asked, sounding surprised.

"His mother did not let him out of her arms for a moment. She healed him. I think she gave up a part of her soul for him."

Hakon's jaw tightened so much at that, he felt as if his teeth would crack. The pain of guilt squeezed him like a fist, his mark burned as if the curse was working. He was not worth giving up anything, let alone the part of a soul. And definitely not a life. And the man who had been responsible for that was still alive.

"That is enough," he said. "You may treat them, Arinborg, after we are wed. If you want to continue, let us get the wedding done first."

The princess studied him for a moment with those big beautiful eyes, her full lips thinning. "All right," she said. "Let's get it over with, Hakon. As you wish."

Solveig glanced at them both, a sly little smile spreading her lips, and Hakon scoffed. Even if Arinborg was a blessing, there was nothing to smile about. One way or the other, the curse would lead to something terrible happening to Arinborg. And he would not be able to protect her. Just as he could not protect his mother.

"Let us go get married," he said. "We need witnesses."

Mia followed Hakon out of the house, his large hand clasped around her smaller one, ensuring she wouldn't make a run for it. Her chest heaved with anxiety.

Outside, the sun had barely risen, and the village was waking up. People carried sacks, hay and wood, cleaned, took animals outside.

Hakon had no idea what he had given Mia along with the permission to help those people. He'd given her back her sense of purpose. The part of her that she had switched off, ignored for the past two and a half years—the part that Dan had bullied her to hide away—came back to the surface and began humming a happy song.

And yet Hakon wanted to control her, another dominant man in her life. She was clearly following the cliché about girls looking for men who reminded them of their father.

Mia remembered her father barking orders at home, as if Mom and Mia were his soldiers. Mom's exhausted face came to mind, the scarf on her head that hid her bald head, the smell of dish soap and burned tuna casserole as she scraped the black remains into the sink. It had burned because Mom had fallen asleep, exhausted after chemo. And yet Dad expected food to be on the table the moment he came home. Mom had died when Mia was fourteen, then Dad's barking had been focused solely on Mia.

She had spent her teenage years taking care of her father. And when she graduated and left San Diego to study medicine in Boston, he never forgave her. Dad had wanted her to stay and take care of him. Moving out was her act of rebellion, her first step towards independence.

And the only one.

Because soon, she'd met Dan.

And now she was under Hakon's control.

She could only imagine what he would do if he realized she

was pretending to be someone else. The real Princess Arinborg could arrive at any moment.

Mia needed to find a way to escape. But until then, she had to keep her cover, keep her baby safe, and survive. That meant going through with this farce of a marriage.

Hakon stopped in front of the great house and turned to face her, grasping her hands. Their eyes locked, and her lips went dry. His pale wolfish eyes held her in place, bright golden-green in the first light of the day.

"People!" Hakon called. "Gather around. Your jarl is being wed."

As people stopped whatever they were doing and circled them, Solveig returned from somewhere with a bunch of white flowers she was turning into a wreath. She approached Mia.

"Here, dear," she said, holding the wreath before herself. "The white crown for the bride. You should have a true wedding, with a white dress, and the blot, and the feast." Solveig threw a reproachful glance at Hakon. "But you can at least wear this wreath for now."

Mia took a deep breath and lowered her head. She straightened her back when the wreath was on her head. Solveig's gesture made her smile.

"Thank you," Mia said.

Mia's hands were still in Hakon's, but she could not look at him. She would marry him, but only because she needed to survive, protect her baby, and find the way out. This plan, to keep pretending she was Arinborg, did not have a happy ending. And the faster she left, the better. Besides, this marriage, under someone else's name, wouldn't be legal anyway.

"Begin, Solveig," Hakon ordered.

Solveig sighed. "Before the gods and before men, let this union be blessed. Freyja and Frigg, bless the bride with good health, with strength to run the household, and with many children to give to Hakon."

Mia's cheeks warmed. If they only knew that wish was closer to coming true than they imagined... What would happen if Hakon found out? Her shoulders tightened. Would he hold the court he was talking about to sentence her and then kill her?

"And may Odin and Thor bless the groom with strength, and health, and many victories to keep peace for the family."

Solveig put a rope over their hands and tied it loosely. Mia's pulse leaped as Hakon's grip tightened.

"Do you, Hakon, take Arinborg as your wife?"

"I do." His voice was curt and low and almost intimate, rich with promise.

"And do you, Arinborg, take Hakon as your husband?"

Mia could not resist it. Her eyes shot to his, and there was heat in them and need and yet restraint. The sudden desire to touch him tingled in her fingertips.

"I do," she said.

Hakon's eyes brightened, and guilt clenched Mia's shoulders till they hurt. She was tricking him. She was pretending to be someone else, but the words came out easily and felt true.

What? Why? *Because I could fall for him, that's why.*

Her skin chilled. No! Falling for him would mean another heartbreak. Falling for him would mean making bad decisions again. Falling for him would mean her mind clouded and emotions taking over.

For the sake of her baby, she could not let it happen.

"Hakon and Arinborg, you are now husband and wife! Kiss!"

The people around them erupted in cheers. Hakon hesitated a moment, as if asking if he could. Mia's lips parted. Was she his wife now?

Despite herself, a small part of her wished Hakon really was her husband, and that he would kiss her. Her pulse jumped.

"Ah, Helheim," Hakon growled, stepped towards her and swept her into his arms. His earthy scent enveloped her, electricity shot through her veins, and his lips covered hers.

CHAPTER SEVEN

As soon as his lips pressed against hers, he knew he was lost. Odin, he had been lost even before.

Even before her yes.

Even before he had touched her for the first time.

She had claimed him the very first moment he saw her by the rune rock.

Her lips were as soft as flower petals, and she smelled like spring, like light, and something airy and flowery.

Delicious.

And like the sea in storm, the need to kiss her, to touch her, to hold her took him and would not let go. Her lips parted, his tongue touched hers, and liquid fire rushed through his veins.

He pressed, sucking her tongue slightly, and she made a low sound in the back of her throat. Forgetting everything, he wrapped his arm around her waist, while his other hand cupped the nape of her neck.

She broke away with a gasp, blinking at him, her green eyes as dark as a pine forest.

She pushed herself off him and took a step back, one hand covering her lips.

Something was wrong. Hakon panted, confused, hot, and abandoned.

Their first kiss, as husband and wife, and she had rejected him. Why?

He was disgusting, that was why. She couldn't bear to look at him much less kiss him.

"Is this what you call not touching me?" She put a hand on the scruff of her neck. "You promised."

All eyes were on them. He glanced at the crowd, and their faces were stern, wide-eyed. Arinborg was about to air their dirty laundry in front of everyone. Yes, he had broken his word not to touch her before she had asked him. So the Beast had shown them how he was going to treat his wife.

Like a beast.

"Not here, woman, to all the gods," he said through gritted teeth. He took her by the arm and led her to his bedchamber. "This is between a husband and his wife."

He fumed with anger, ignoring her protests.

It was one thing that she detested the idea of being intimate with him. It was quite another that she had shown it publicly.

But why did he care? They all saw the beast in him.

As soon as he shut the door to the bedchamber, he turned to her.

"Are you that arrogant, Princess?"

She gasped. "Arrogant? You said—"

"I know what I said. And I stick to my word. But a husband kisses his wife at their wedding. And I did not do anything you did not seem to enjoy."

Her face reddened like a bloody sunset. "That's not true. I didn't agree—"

He covered the space between them, pinning her to the wall, between his arms. She watched him, shocked. So delicate, so beautiful. How he longed to kiss those soft lips again. "You agreed, Arinborg. You agreed to be my wife. And a wife does not humiliate her husband in front of his own people. You should not have pushed me off like that in front of everyone, as if I had forced myself upon you against your will."

Tears streamed down her cheeks, but she was still holding his gaze like a warrior. He looked her up and down, carefully. Why was she crying? Did he frighten her? Or did she have another reason? Had something happened to her? The thought made him want to kill someone.

"People might call me a beast," he said. "But I already told you—"

"Men. You all *tell*, don't you. Talk is cheap, Hakon."

She might as well have kicked him right in the gut. And just as he had found what he wanted to say, someone knocked on the door and he stepped away from her.

Solveig stood in the door opening, her face worried. "Jarl. Mistress. Two more babes are coughing, plus one more child and two women have started."

Arinborg paled. "It's an epidemic."

Hakon frowned. Another magical word he did not understand.

The princess headed towards the door. "You said I could treat the sick after we were married."

He rushed after her.

"Where are *you* going?" she asked.

"I am the jarl and these people are my responsibility. I am coming to see what can be done to help them."

The three of them rushed towards the hospital, as Mia had begun to call it in her head. They went as fast as Solveig's bad leg allowed. Mia made a mental note to look at it later when she had a chance.

Mia was married now. Well, not technically, of course. The marriage was not real.

But the kiss...

The kiss was real. His lips, soft and hard, giving and probing...Hakon electrified her whole body. He'd made her fly. Sent her pulse into the stratosphere. Until he'd touched her there, at the back of her neck.

The same place Dan used to grab when he wanted to discipline her.

Memories washed over her like a cold shower.

No more kissing Hakon. No matter how attractive he was.

She needed to think about her patients. Hakon wanted to help them. To help her. Didn't he have some Viking stuff to do?

But he was worried, she could see that, and it warmed her heart.

Wheezing, desperate, sucking coughs filled the hospital that was now more crowded. Mia's blood chilled as she saw a mother cradling a baby whose thin little voice broke with the whoops of suffocation.

Mia rushed to them. The baby must be just six months old. She was coughing nonstop, in that cute baby-cough, except when she wanted to breathe in, she couldn't. All she could do was to try to suck in air with that terrible *whoop* sound that allowed very little air in. The baby began opening and closing her mouth, unable to take a breath. Her lips turned slightly blue.

"Shhh." Mia stroked her belly gently, then looked at her mother. "You need to put her on her belly and slap her on the back so that she can cough the mucus out."

The frightened mother did as she was asked, but the baby was still struggling to breathe. Mia slapped her quickly on the back. "It's okay, you can take that breath now."

Everyone stilled. Even the other coughing patients.

Mia counted seconds in her head. The baby tried to suck in air.

One. Nothing.

Two. Still gaping.

Three.

The baby breathed in and began coughing out the mucous, then cried. Her mother sighed out in relief, tears filling her eyes.

She hoped the mother would stay healthy for as long as possible. Whooping cough epidemics had been common before widespread immunization. And though it was more dangerous in children, more adults would also soon be sick with the one-hundred-day cough, as it was known.

Mia glanced at Solveig and Hakon. "The whole village will be sick soon. Only those who have had it will stay strong. Babies will be the ones in the biggest danger. I need help. We need firewood, water, herbs, and food."

Hakon gave a stern nod, his pale eyes as concerned as ever.

He opened the front door and bellowed, "Hey! Frogeir! Torfi! Come here!"

When the two men appeared, Hakon said, "Whatever Princess Arinborg needs, you do for her. Even if she tells you to ride your horse to the sun."

Mia pursed her lips. The way Hakon had barked orders just now—he'd sounded exactly like Dan. Controlling, overwhelming, violent Dan.

And yet, Hakon did not mean to control or overwhelm or dominate *her*. He barked and ordered people around to help the sick.

Mia studied him, torn between feeling angry with him and being impressed by his readiness to do anything for his people.

"Save the people, Arinborg," Hakon said.

Mia nodded. "Maybe I have something that might help in my purse. Can the three of you bring more firewood and water for now?"

Hakon nodded and walked away with his men. She pulled the strap over her neck and turned away so that no one would see what she had, then opened her purse.

There was an almost-full bottle of Tylenol. Good. She'd crush the pills and only give the powder to those with high fever. And she'd need to be careful with the dosages to the babies—the wrong dosage might be toxic for their little livers.

She resumed her search. There was a makeup case, a manicure set, her wallet, a hairbrush, a couple of Band-Aids, her e-reader, her now-useless phone. She also found a couple of pens, a few elastic hair bands, a scarf, sunglasses, and a dead glow-in-the-dark bracelet she'd been given at a club Dan had insisted they go to a couple of weeks ago. She stared at the liquid moving inside the plastic tube as her mind drifted to that night, how she'd put on a smile and tried to play her role as the happy girlfriend. How she'd tried not to let Dan see that she wasn't drinking.

Forcing herself back to her current role play, she quickly closed the purse. She'd have to keep the contents out of sight or it would be clear she didn't belong here. She could crush the pills without anyone seeing them, but the rest...they could be the things that betrayed her. She would need to hide them well.

CHAPTER EIGHT

"You should go, Hakon." Mia was cutting herbs at the table by the hearth in the hospital. "You might get sick."

After a couple of hours, the house was even louder with coughs and whoops, but Mia was glad they were all under one roof. Pertussis was highly contagious, and she needed to limit its spread as much as possible. Eleven people were already sick, including two babies, two toddlers, three older children, two women, and two men.

"Torfi! Bring more water," Hakon barked, then glanced at her with a frown. "You might get sick, too."

"It's unlikely," she said. She had been vaccinated, of course. When she started her residency program, she had been checked for the state of her immunization, and the pertussis vaccine had still been working. So, most likely, she was safe to treat the sick. Her baby would be okay, too. No research showed any influence of whooping cough on a growing fetus.

"Why?"

"Because I already had it." It was as close to the truth as she could get.

Mia finished cutting onion and threw the bits into a bowl with honey and garlic for the antibacterial mixture. The cooks in the great hall had begun preparing the stew Mia had described to Solveig. Another girl had been sent out in the woods to gather more meadowsweet. The patients in the hospital would soon chew through Solveig's reserves. Mia planned to crush the Tylenol later in the evening, when she would have some privacy.

"So did I," Hakon said.

"For you, it was a long time ago. Your body..." she looked for the appropriate words to describe waning immunization. "Might have forgotten how to fight it."

He chuckled. "My body would never forget how to fight." He turned to Torfi, who had appeared at the door, took the buckets of water from him and began filling the cauldron to set the water to boil.

Now that Mia's mixture was complete, she would have to make sure the sick took it regularly.

There was not enough honey for a larger batch, so more servants went out to look for it. They'd probably need to fight that bear. Thankfully, there was plenty of wild garlic and onion. They had excellent natural antibacterial qualities. Mia wished now that she had learned more about herbalism and natural remedies. She had always been fascinated by them and had read more about them than her classmates in medical school. But there was still so much she didn't know.

She couldn't believe how fast time flew. Eventually, her patients were all taken care of, and she knew she would do everything in her power to help them. Satisfaction from her work made her body buzz as if she had a whole swarm of bees inside of her. Lightness filled her and a smile touched her lips. She missed doing what she loved.

"It is time for dagmal, Arinborg," Hakon said. "You will eat with me."

Mia's stomach growled at the thought of food. She wanted to protest his commanding tone, but all the patients were fed and taken care of, and she could use a break. Plus, she needed to eat for her baby's sake.

Mia followed Hakon. Daylight hurt her eyes after hours in the semidarkness of the windowless hospital. The chirping of birds and gentle rustling of leaves from the woods behind the village were a welcome change.

"Is this how it's going to be, Hakon?" Mia said. "You bossing me around? Do you know you sound exactly like my Dad?"

And like Dan. But mentioning another man to an angry Viking husband seemed like a bad idea.

She continued walking, but after a few steps realized he wasn't following. She turned around. He stood looking at her in a way that made her want to run.

Hakon's face was destruction. It was death itself.

He covered the space between them in three giant steps. He loomed over her, and even though he didn't touch her, he pinned Mia to the ground. "*Never* say that again. I am *nothing* like your father."

He meant Arinborg's father, of course. And she couldn't help wanting to know why he was so full of hatred for his bride's father. "You are not the only one who feels like that about my Dad," she said truthfully. "But what did he do to *you*?"

Hakon squeezed his lips so tight they whitened. "There will be no talk of that. Not a word. Or I swear to Odin, I will kill someone."

His eyes became dark, almost amber, his pupils dilated from all the adrenaline that must be fountaining in his blood right now. Mia swallowed. "All right, all right. I won't ask again."

He turned around and walked towards the great house. Mia followed him, watching his back, which was so broad, children could play soccer on it. His waist and hips were narrow, and under his clothes, strong muscles moved. Mia's eyes fell on his round ass, and her gaze jumped away, her cheeks stinging. What was wrong with her? She should not be interested in his ass!

Despite his outburst, curiosity burned her. Something bad had happened between Hakon and Arinborg's father. Maybe it had to do with his temper. Mia had seen his good side. He was a kind man. He had given up his house to be used as a hospital. But he had so much anger inside.

"Why are you like this, Hakon? Why do you have this need to tell me and everyone else what to do? Why do you want to make people afraid of you?"

The gaze he leveled on her was so heavy she thought she'd fall under its weight. "Because it is the only way I can make them keep distance from me."

There was so much pain in his voice that Mia held her breath. "What do you mean? You help your people. Your warriors listen to you—"

"Only because I am the Beast. Unstoppable. I protect my men. They respect me as a warrior, as a leader. Haven't you heard about me? Your father wants me for himself, to fight for him."

Something deep in Mia ached at his words. He was a strong man who could snap her in half if he wanted. She had no doubt he was a great warrior. But to call himself the Beast? She itched to touch him, to make the pain in his voice go away.

Hakon stopped in front of the gates to the great house. He looked up and Mia followed his eyes. Above them, right under the roof, were broad gables, and on them, long, interwoven carvings of wolves with snarling jaws.

"Why are we looking up there?" she said.

"Haven't you heard about the curse?"

Mia frowned, a million questions popping into her head. But he'd already entered the hall, and when she followed him, the morning meal was underway. The hall was full of warriors sitting at the long wooden tables, and the room hummed with the voices of fifty or so men and the taps of spoons against bowls and knives against boards. Around them, servants delivered food and poured drinks. The air was thick with the smell of cooked meat and vegetables. Hakon headed towards the table that stood at the head of the hall.

Mia felt a little uneasy as the eyes of so many armed men fell on her. It reminded her of every time Dan took her anywhere; he always had at least two bodyguards, who looked at her in the same way—a combination of respect and caution. She was their boss's favorite toy, and they had to protect her with their lives but also follow her every step, and kill her if Dan told them to.

What was the relationship between Hakon and these men? Were they like his army, his warband, or his employees? He had to feed them, that was obvious. Mia itched to ask, but that was surely something a Viking princess should know. Did a meal like this happen every day, or was it a special occasion?

But even more than that, Mia longed to find out more about the curse. Hakon sat at the head table, and Mia supposed that she needed to take a place next to him as his wife, although she would rather find a quiet corner where no one would look at her or talk to her for a while. Hakon watched her as she took her seat, and Mia felt his eyes on her like a pair of red-hot rods scorching her skin.

The table under her fingers was smooth and cool, while the

air in the room was warm. Or was it just her? The servants brought the stew—the stew she had ordered for the sick. "Hey!" Mia called the servant girl. "Come here! Is there any more of this left? We need it for the sick in the hospital."

"We served all of it, mistress. I did not know. No one told us."

Hakon's face distorted in anger, and the girl's face was a mask of complete horror, as if he was about to breath fire on her. He opened his mouth to say something, but Mia interrupted him.

"It's all right. It's all right. Probably just a miscommunication. What's your name?"

As she said the words, she knew she took on, yet again, the role of mediator. Growing up, that was what she had done. She'd learned that from her mother, and then when she was gone, Mia had taken on that role to keep her father's temper at bay.

And then Dan. Even when things had been bad between them, Mia had been the only one who could gently, without undermining his authority, calm him down.

Mia shook internally from the memories, but that was who she was. She made things easier.

"My name is Lifa," the girl answered.

"Start making another one, Lifa, just like this one. Bring me something else to eat and do not touch my bowl. I'll take the stew to the hospital."

"Yes, mistress." She shot one more frightened glance at Hakon and retreated.

He followed her, his face still a threat.

"Like that." Mia gestured at him. "Why do you need to be so frightening? She's already terrified."

He studied her, his golden-green eyes surprised. "Are *you* not terrified?"

That was a good question. She had been when he had swept her onto his horse and brought her to the village. But something deep inside of her told her that there was no reason to be terrified of a man who would give up his house for the sick and help her in any way he could. He had also promised not to touch her until she asked him to. And she believed him.

"I don't know," Mia said, looking into his eyes a little longer than she had intended to.

"You should be." His deep voice brushed against her ears, electrifying even the softest, invisible fuzz on her skin. "I am not going to be a husband who brings you happiness. I do not bring people anything but sorrow."

CHAPTER NINE

She is mine.

Hakon had thought that every day for the past week as he'd watched Arinborg—the woman with hair the color of young honey, eyes like the first grass in spring, and a mouth as sweet as mead from Valhalla. She was his wife. She was his by law and before the gods.

But he could not do anything to make her his in bed.

He had promised her, and he would not break his word. Not to her.

The need to earn her trust, to have her smile at him became stronger than the burning that set his blood on fire every night as she was preparing to sleep. He had to turn his back to her while she was changing into her night shift, and the whisper of clothes against her skin, the creak of the bed as she lay in it tortured him.

She was his wife. And yet he could not touch her.

Every night, she was just one step away, sleeping in his bed, cuddled in his furs. He lay on the floor on the sheepskins by the end of the bed. Hakon thought how those furs brushed her skin, and he wished he could touch her instead.

Her peaceful breathing as she slept made his heart beat calmer. She had the rare ability to fall asleep almost at once as soon as she lay in bed. It must be exhaustion from treating the sick all day long. She also ate as much and as hungrily as a man, and yet she was as thin as a teenage girl.

In the week since their wedding, more people had become sick. All nine babes in the village were now in the hospital, as Arinborg called it, with their mothers, coughing, vomiting and turning red and blue. Arinborg was most worried about one baby who did not suck much of the milk and began weakening.

As Hakon watched the dark ceiling of the bedroom, he thought that something was very odd about Arinborg. It was the little things. How she refused to eat using just her hands and a knife like everyone else and ordered a small pitchfork from the blacksmith to eat meat and cooked vegetables. She refused to drink mead or ale and only drank water. She demanded to wash daily, not on Saturdays like all Norsemen. For the first few days, she refused to wear anything other than the rich dress she had arrived in. She'd only agreed to accept the clothes that Solveig gave her after her clothes had torn and become filthy from her work in the hospital.

She was a princess, so she was spoiled. But she worked hard, and she was not squeamish about cleaning vomit, snot, dirty diapers, and the contents of the night pots. Hakon could not help but admire Arinborg's skills, care, and hard work. All that was so different from what he had assumed Nyr's daughter would be like.

But when Arinborg had put on the dress of a townswoman, something had exploded in his chest, as if a rock had broken away from the mountain and a waterfall of warm, clear water had begun flowing down the slope. She looked like home in that simple white linen tunic and pale-blue woolen apron dress fastened by two silver brooches on her chest. Hakon imagined, despite himself, how she'd welcome him home after a raid, with a huge smile on her face and a horn of mead in her hands. Just like his mother had always welcomed his father.

But all that would never be.

He disgusted her, and she did not want a real marriage with him. And even if one day he would lay with her to give her children, she would never forgive him after she learned of his plans for her father.

But hurting her feelings could not stop his revenge. When that worm had taken away the only person who had not seen a curse in him, he had taken away the only good thing in Hakon's life. He had taken away part of his soul. Revenge alone would satisfy Hakon. Perhaps then he could forgive himself for his mother's death.

And despite the pestilence in the village, Hakon needed his allies. Secretly, he sent a messenger to the three jarls that he knew were against King Nyr's spreading power. Jarl Rafr was more to the north and was rumored to be next on Nyr's path of conquest. Jarl Brunn was to the south and was himself interested in becoming a king, and Hakon would rather serve him than the man who got what he wanted through lies and schemes. And Jarl Vefuss was the oldest of the men, and he came from the old generation of Norsemen who valued independence and strength above all. He would rather die than let someone dictate to him who he and his children fought for.

Hakon invited them for a feast in two moons to discuss the plan of attack.

That night at dinner, he watched Arinborg's beautiful, delicate hand operate the small pitchfork and put a juicy piece of roasted meat in her mouth. He watched her full lips move as she chewed it, her eyes closing briefly in bliss. He let out a long breath to calm the fire that began to seethe in his loins.

The hall was not as full as usual—two more houses had been claimed as hospitals, and Arinborg had a small band of women who were still standing to help her nurse the sick. Twenty men and women, and almost all children and babies in the village were in the hospitals. But so far, no one had died.

"I will have a feast in two moons," Hakon said. "I need you to prepare the best one you can."

Arinborg looked up at him. "A feast? What can I do about it? I don't have time—you know how busy I am at the hospital."

His eyebrows rose. "You are a jarl's wife. It is your duty to be a good hostess. It is as if you were raised in another world, Arinborg. Are these things not clear to you?"

She paled, and her mouth stopped moving. "Yes. You're right."

"I did not say anything until now about you not fulfilling your duties of the head of the household—managing servants and thralls, preparing food and drinks, making clothes—because you are busy with the hospital. But you said in one moon they won't be able to pass the sickness anymore. In two moons, people either heal or die, and I will have guests because I must."

"Why?"

Hakon clenched his jaws. "That is not a woman's business. I am the jarl, and I need other jarls as friends. Your business is to be a good hostess and make the guests feel welcome. Did your mother not teach you that?"

Arinborg pursed her lips. "She did. But if you talk to your guests the same way you are talking to me, then your mother taught you even less."

Her mentioning his mother set his world into a net of sharp

blades that moved and cut his body into thin slices. "Do not dare say a bad word about my mother."

She laid down her small pitchfork and looked him straight in the eye.

"Hakon, if you don't want people to think you are a beast, don't behave like one."

He froze, the air knocked out of him as if she had just kicked him in the gut. "You don't know what you are talking about," he growled.

She lay her hand on his, and a wave of warmth covered him like a blanket. "Is it because of your birthmark? Anyone would feel a little shy, but you have nothing to worry about—"

"Hold your tongue. That does not concern you."

"Hakon, it's just that I can't help but see it. Your people are afraid of you, and I'm not sure if they have a real reason for that. You bark at them, but you do take care of them. I think you do more for them than they realize. Why are they really afraid?"

Images filled his mind: winter; the door of this great mead hall opening; his dead mother in his arms; her body frozen, torn by wolves. His father jumping to his feet, face whiter than the snow. King Nyr's eyes as wide as two moons. And all eyes in the mead hall—servants, farmers, children, warriors—on him. Same terror in them. Same revulsion.

There was nothing that a Viking was more afraid of than bad luck.

Not even death.

And Hakon had been born with it, right on his face.

"Every Norseman knows why they are afraid of me. The real question, Princess, is why aren't you?"

CHAPTER TEN

Mia swallowed a hard knot.

The fire in the small oil lamps that hung around the room threw dim orange light on Hakon's face, playing like little fires in his eyes, making him look devilish, violent. Dangerous.

So dangerous that the fear she had not felt in a week gripped her stomach again with an ice-cold fist.

Had she made another mistake? Had she done something else that gave her away?

Her hand landed on her belly.

"Why are you not afraid of the curse?" he repeated.

"The curse?"

"The curse." He pointed at his birthmark.

Mia frowned. "Wait. Do you think you are cursed because of your birthmark?"

His gaze lay heavy on her. "Of course. All know this. Did you not?"

Mia swore under her breath. She wished she had read more about Vikings. Should everyone know that? She went with, "No. I knew."

"Why do you appear surprised then?"

She raised her chin. "Just because I know, doesn't mean I believe it."

The astonishment on his face was priceless. "You do not?" His voice sounded as if he had eaten gravel instead of stew.

"No. There's absolutely no proof of that. How exactly would a congenital, benign irregularity on skin lead to whatever you call a *curse*?"

Hakon looked at her as though he could eat her alive. "You are saying your magical words again."

One of these days Mia really needed to start speaking like a proper Viking.

"Sorry. I just mean, your birthmark is the same skin, just a different color. It's not a curse. It has no purpose, and it's a completely random thing that happened. Trust me. I'm a healer. If anything, it makes you look…"

She wanted to say *mysterious, badass, unforgettable* but stopped herself. She should not give him compliments or other ideas that she might feel more for him than she wanted to.

Plus, she didn't.

She didn't!

During the past few days, every time she had thought about him, a lightness had filled her chest. He hadn't left her side. Of course, he still didn't trust her. But he also helped in the hospital. Sometimes Mia needed him to run an errand, and he did what she asked without hesitation. The more people who got sick, the fewer servants there were to do household tasks. Hakon served the stew and medicine, took laundry and dishes to the well, brought firewood and water, vegetables and meat for cooking.

Mia's pulse always made a little leap when she heard his voice or felt his presence, as if feathers brushed her skin.

"It makes me look what?" Hakon said. His voice gained that

velvety quality again, and sweat broke through her skin at the back of her neck.

She looked at her hands. "It doesn't make you look ugly," she said and coughed. "If that's what you're worried about, you shouldn't be."

She still didn't look at him. He was doing that thing again; his gaze was scorching her skin.

"You do not think I am ugly?" His voice, coarse and low now, vibrated against her skin.

"No," she said. Why had she said that? All air left the room. "But that doesn't matter, does it?"

She met his gaze and regretted it. His eyes were so dark, they were almost brown. He looked at her as though she held all the pain and anguish in the world in her hands and was about to decide what to do with it. "What if it does?"

Her mouth felt as dry as paper. "I thought this marriage was not about happiness for you."

"It was not. What is it about for you?"

She swallowed. "Survival."

He frowned. "Survival? Is he—" Hakon's face became so livid he choked on the words. "Is he threatening you? Your father?"

"No! No. He isn't. I just meant, in general. For a woman—" Mia shouldn't have blurted the word "survival" out loud. She was out of her depth, improvising, and she hoped she was headed in the right direction. "As a woman, you leave your father's house, go to your husband's. You depend on him. On men. So, it's survival. My life kind of depends on you, doesn't it?"

And not just her life. Her baby's, too. Oh god. How would Hakon react if he found out about her pregnancy? A chill prickled her skin. He would probably be furious. Disappointed. Feel betrayed. But something deep inside her now knew that he wouldn't hurt her no matter how he felt, and the realization released a small knot of tension in her gut.

Hakon cocked his head. "I suppose so. Did you finish your dinner? How did the whole pig's leg fit into your stomach?"

Mia coughed, a little embarrassed. She'd had a crazy appetite ever since she'd gone into her second trimester a week ago. "Yes, finished."

"Come, I want to give you something."

Hakon offered her his hand, and Mia put her palm in his. Whereas in the beginning she had been terrified, now she accepted his touch without hesitation. A buzz ran through her veins. His skin was always warm and dry, a little calloused, and pleasant. His big strong hand wrapped around hers made excitement bubble up in the pit of her stomach.

Hakon led her towards the bedroom, and Mia tensed. "Why are we going there?"

"Arinborg, we have been sleeping in that room for a week now, and I have not lifted a finger to touch you."

In the bedroom, the fire burned, the air was warm and pleasant. The whole week whenever they had been in the bedroom together, she'd been aware of his every movement until her head touched the pillow and she passed out from exhaustion. But now something changed; she had never felt like this. Even though Mia's feet were tired and she ached to lie down, the electricity in the air made all the hair stand up on Mia's skin.

"I have a gift for you," Hakon said, and moved to one of the chests standing by the wall. He rummaged there, the muscles of his broad back rolling under his tunic. Then he turned to Mia with something in his hands.

It was some kind of white fur, maybe arctic fox or mink. It looked rich and absolutely gorgeous.

Hakon looked at it with anguish, briefly closed his eyes,

opened them again and glanced at her. He held out his hands with the furs to her.

"This is for you."

Mia took the bundle and saw that it was a cloak with a hood—long and broad, and so soft, Mia wanted to brush it against her cheek.

"The cloak belonged to my mother," Hakon said. "I never gave you a wedding present. You deserve so much more than a fur cloak. You are a princess. You are the most skilled healer I have ever known. And you are—"

He cut himself off, and the urge to find out became so strong in Mia, she wanted to pull the word out of his mouth.

"I am what?"

"You are the most beautiful woman I have ever seen."

Mia stopped breathing. Her heart began pounding so hard, the warriors in the great hall must have heard it.

"I can't accept this, Hakon." Her voice sounded like the creak of an old hinge.

"No? I also have her jewelry—"

"No! No! I don't mean it's not enough. I mean, it's too much. Her things must mean a lot to you."

Mia sat on the edge of the bed, her legs beginning to feel wobbly.

"Please, Arinborg. I want you to have it. She would want that."

Tears blurred Mia's vision. "Thank you."

Hakon pointed at the cloak in Mia's hands. "There's a brooch to fasten it. My father had it made from the hacksilver and amber he got on his first raid."

Mia brushed her hand across the fur and felt the cold metal of the brooch. It was big and round like a small Viking shield, with amber in the middle. Around the stone, patterns of dotted, interwoven branches and beasts curved.

Mia's fingers trembled a little. "It's breathtaking." Her throat clenched. "What was your mother's name?"

"Dota." Hakon looked at his hands.

"What a beautiful name. Tell me about her."

Hakon's face fell, then tensed so much Mia thought she saw his bones sharpen through his skin. "I haven't talked about her since she died."

"How old were you?"

"Twelve winters."

"Twelve winters... That's young."

The ache of losing her own mother at fourteen still pierced Mia's heart. Was Arinborg's mother alive? Without knowing, she couldn't share her own pain with Hakon.

"What was she like?" Mia asked.

Hakon sat on the edge of the bed next to her and did not respond for a while, staring into the distance. "She smelled of meadowsweet. Her hair was golden. She liked to laugh. She was strong. And she loved my father. She was the only one who did not think I was cursed."

Mia squeezed the fur in her hands, wishing she could meet Dota. Hakon's eyes locked with Mia's, and his were burning.

"You are the second person who does not think that."

Mia swallowed and lowered her gaze. "Dota was a smart woman, then."

Hakon chuckled softly. "She would have liked you."

Mia smiled, and for the first time in a very long time, she did not feel like she wanted to run anywhere.

"What happened to her?"

The warmth left his face as if she had hit him. Hakon stood up, went to the chest and closed it.

"Enough stories for today. Time to go to sleep."

His rejection stung a little, although she knew it was for the best. She had seen yet a new side to Hakon, and the gesture of giving her his mother's cloak meant so much to him. And to her.

Good job keeping your distance, she chided herself as they were doing their ritual of Hakon standing with his back to her as she changed into her night gown.

"Done," said Mia while diving into the softness of the bed full of furs.

Hakon turned to her, and Mia's favorite part of the evening began.

It was called *shirtless Hakon*.

Hidden in between folds of the furs so that Hakon wouldn't see, Mia watched him. He removed his tunic, and the canyons of his muscles showed, his smooth skin glistening in the dancing firelight from the hearth. His shoulders and biceps were like rocks. His six-pack and the V of his side muscles were sculpted in smooth lines. And his pecs were broad and strong. Her fingers itched to touch the light layer of blond hair on his chest. Hakon glanced at her, and she shut her eyes.

Mia heard him lie on the floor. He breathed unevenly, so he wasn't asleep yet. Talking about his mother had obviously upset him, and Mia wanted to comfort him, to feel his strong arms around her, his warmth on her skin. She yearned to hug and kiss him.

But she wouldn't. That would be the beginning of a disaster.

"Hakon," she said.

"Hm?"

"Come to bed."

She heard a quick rustle of the sheepskin. "What?"

Mia rose on one elbow and looked at him. His face showed alarm.

"Come sleep in bed, next to me."

"Do you want to—"

"No! Not *that*. You've been sleeping on the floor ever since I arrived. I doubt you sleep well there. You must be exhausted. Just lie here, next to me. You can't touch me though, all right?"

Hakon's eyes darkened. "I do not know if I can restrict myself, Princess."

Mia's eyes widened. "Oh... Then forget it."

"No. I will come."

He stood up, his muscles thick and powerful, and walked to the other side of the bed. Without breaking eye contact, he climbed in and covered himself with the fur blanket. Mia turned her back to him, breathing heavily.

"Good night," she said.

He didn't respond for a while, then said in a coarse voice, "Good night."

And even though she did not see it, she could feel his gaze burning into her back and her whole body flooded with warmth. She was playing with fire. And everyone knew how those games ended.

CHAPTER ELEVEN

ANOTHER WEEK of torture had passed, Hakon sleeping in his bed with Arinborg by his side but unable to touch her. She had been exhausted every day after taking care of about half of the village. All of the children and babies were now sick, but Arinborg had allowed the first three to go back home, claiming that the worst for them was over and they could not pass the disease anymore.

Arinborg slept on her side, facing him. One hand lay on the pillow, palm up, and he suppressed the urge to place his hand in hers just to feel her warmth and softness. Her face looked peaceful and so beautiful, long lashes framing her closed eyelids. Her lips, round and softened in sleep, looked so inviting.

Hakon growled as he was trying to fall asleep, refusing to look down where he would probably see the curve of her breast under the night shift.

The gods must be laughing at him because the person he felt the closest to was his enemy's daughter. He wanted to give her everything she had ever wanted. But he was about to rob her of her father, and the thought gnawed at his gut like a hungry dog.

He climbed out of bed and walked through the quiet mead hall, then outside into the coolness of the night. He was restless, his muscles burning with the need for her. Gods, how he wished things were different between them.

Later that day, in the hospital, Hakon was pouring water into a cauldron to boil and Arinborg was giving a child honey and garlic water.

A babe that lay in a crib stirred and began a coughing fit. Hakon looked around to see if its mother would come to soothe it, but no one came.

"Hakon, can you please take Mette?" Arinborg asked.

Hakon drew his mouth into a straight line. "Her mother will not be happy if she sees me with her babe."

Arinborg grimaced. "Nonsense. We need to make sure the baby doesn't suffocate from mucus. You need to hold her straight. Come on."

Hakon clenched his jaws and put the bucket he was holding on the floor, but still did not take a step towards the baby. He was the nightmare people scared their children with. "What if I pass it on?"

Little Mette continued coughing, and her face turning bluish.

"You're not sick and she already is. Come on, you see she's struggling."

"Not the disease. The curse."

Arinborg frowned at him. "There. Is. No. Curse! Now take that baby before it's too late!"

Hakon hurried towards the crib and took the babe in his arms. She was so fragile, so small and tense, her little body shaking from the coughing spasms.

"Hold her vertically, slightly inclined forward, so that it's easier for her to cough out the mucus," Arinborg instructed.

Hakon felt like a bear with a kitten in its paws. "Will I not squeeze her to death?"

"No! Have you never held a baby?"

"No."

"You'll be fine. Quickly, do as I say. Slap her on her back, not too hard, though, to help mucus come out."

Hakon held the babe straight and inclined it slightly forward as Arinborg had told him. He patted her back, but she continued to cough, desperate. Then she stopped. She gulped for air but could not take a breath. Her lips turned blue. Fear the likes of which he had not even felt on the battlefield gripped his gut in its cold claws.

"She doesn't breathe," he mumbled.

"Talk to her. Slap her back a little harder."

He did as she said, probably slapping too hard, then softer. "Breathe, Mette. For Freya and for Odin, breathe."

The babe sucked in the air with a thin *whoop* sound and cried. He pressed her warm little body against his ribcage, still holding her upright. "Good girl. The gods are with you. Breathe now. You are all right."

"See, that wasn't so bad."

Arinborg finished with the child she had been busy with and went to the next one.

Hakon gave a relieved laugh. "I suppose not. I almost shit myself."

Arinborg laughed, too. "You did well. You are good with babies."

Hakon wanted to reply that he was not, but the door opened and a woman entered, her eyes as wide as armrings. It was Oda, Mette's mother. "Get away from my baby, Beast!" she yelled as she rushed towards him.

Shame washed over Hakon like an icy wave in a storm, as if he had done something wrong.

The woman took the babe away from him and curled over it with her back to him, like she thought he would throw himself on her.

"Oda," Arinborg said. "He was just comforting her. She had a fit—"

"No! He cannot touch the babies. It is bad enough that he is our jarl. He will curse her."

Arinborg stopped giving the healing water to the child and stood up, her eyes throwing lightning bolts.

"He what?"

She walked slowly towards the woman.

"He will curse her. Like he is cursed,"

"You stop this nonsense at once," Arinborg said. "He's not cursed. No one is cursed. He has probably saved your baby's life. There was no one around and Mette needed to be held."

"I just went to the privy."

"I know. That's not the point. He didn't curse your baby. Stop saying that. All of you." Arinborg turned to look around the hospital. There were several dozen people there; some of them slept, but many listened. "You're all lucky to have Hakon Ulfsson as your jarl. He is doing everything for you. He gave up his own house so that all of you can heal faster. If anything, his mark is the sign of a blessing."

"You are protecting him, Princess," Oda said while rocking the baby. "I understand. He is your husband. And we are all grateful for you, for you healing skills. But do you know what he did to his mother?"

Pain pierced Hakon, as if Oda had just peeled off his skin. Arinborg frowned.

"No," she said. "But I'm sure whatever happened was not his fault."

"But it was. He cursed her—that is what happened."

Arinborg glanced at him, her eyes questioning. Hakon felt helpless. He had never wanted her to find out. Let alone this way. If she did, he might lose the second person in this world who was kind to him.

But it seemed that the time had come.

"Come, Princess. I'll tell you."

He offered her his hand, and she studied it.

"Don't go, mistress," Oda said. "I'm fearing for you."

That seemed to have done it. Arinborg rolled her eyes and put her hand in his. "Let's go. I'm not afraid, and you shouldn't be either, Oda."

Hakon did not think he had ever held anything so precious as her hand. He led her to the longhouse and asked the servants to bring bread, cheese, butter, and water, since he knew she would not drink mead or ale. He took a few sheepskins, his cloak, and Arinborg's arctic fox cloak.

"Where are we going?" Arinborg asked.

"You will see. We will need to spend the night there. Do you think the hospital can spare you for one night?"

Arinborg looked back towards where the hospital was. "I suppose they would be all right for one night."

"Good. I have not taken anyone there before. You will love it. Do you trust me?"

Her answer suddenly became more important than taking his next breath. She studied him with a frown, but then her features smoothed. She smiled, and her smile was the most beautiful thing he had ever seen.

"I do."

A giant iceberg thawed in his chest. The servants brought their things, and Hakon put the rolls of sheepskins on his back and a travel purse with food on his belt.

"Let us be on our way. It is a bit of a hike."

Arinborg smiled and followed him, and as they were approaching the mountain that had been his escape since his mother had died, happiness flooded his whole being. But the thought of sharing the tale of the worst night of his life invaded that happiness like raiders landing on a vulnerable shore.

CHAPTER TWELVE

Mia thought her chest would burst. They had been hiking for about one hour now, and even though she was only fifteen weeks pregnant, the strain took more out of her than she had thought it would.

When Hakon announced that they had finally arrived, she whispered, "hallelujah." His arched brow said he'd heard her.

And it wasn't even the top of the mountain. Hakon led her into a little clearing between the pines and boulders.

The clearing was a combination of rocks that formed a natural balcony without rails, and it protruded into the air with nothing but a rocky mountain slope under it. When they stepped onto it, the darkening sky seemed so close that if she stretched her arms, she could touch it. And the air felt so fresh she could almost drink it. Down below was the fjord, winding like a wide blue serpent among the mountains. To the right, in a little valley, was Lomdalen. It looked like a miniature toy village, the houses dark with yellowish roofs. Smoke rose from some of the homes as dinner was prepared. And Mia could see tiny people and animals move from up here.

It was colder here, too, and she cuddled into Dota's cloak, thankful for it.

But everything she saw around her—the fjord, the mountains, the forest—all that paled in comparison to Hakon. She had trusted him to lead her without knowing where they were going. She hated that his own people were blinded by superstitions and prejudice. How could they not see how good he was, how kind? There was not an ounce of curse in him. If anything, he was a blessing.

But he had promised to tell her what happened to his mother.

"You were right," Mia said. "I love it."

Hakon turned and looked directly at her. She had never seen his face so soft, so peaceful. The wolfish look was gone. He was now a giant, gorgeous man who was free. Mia stilled, as if afraid to scare off a wild animal.

He was smiling.

The world shifted, and the balance was as fragile as a soap bubble, and she didn't want to burst it. It was not a wide smile, nothing like an all-American boy. It was a half-smile, but it made his face look magical.

Human.

Magnificent.

"When my mother was gone, this is where I came to hide. I could still see them from here. But this is also where I was free from them."

Mia's eyes blurred. "A place to hide. A luxury I never had." Not back home in San Diego and not in Boston with Dan.

Hakon gestured around him. "You can have it now."

Mia smiled, and a tear crawled down her cheek.

She could have it now.

With Hakon.

"Thank you," she said.

Hakon removed the sheepskins from his back.

"I spent much time here, thinking, away from them. From their glances full of fear and blame." He laid the sheepskins on the ground. "I shall start a fire. It is going to get cold soon."

When the fire was crackling, chasing away the descending night, Mia and Hakon sat on the sheepskins and watched the dancing flames. Mia itched to ask him about his mother, but she stopped herself. She knew all too well about secrets.

"That night, she woke me up," he said, looking at the flames. "I still remember the cold of the winter mead hall and how I did not want to go anywhere. She gave me an ax. A grown-up's ax. I had never held a true battle ax before." He chuckled. "It was too heavy for me, but I did not let her see that."

Hakon split a twig and threw it into the fire.

"My father stood between us and the doors. He looked at me as if my head had turned into that of a snake. It was the first time that he held my gaze for longer than the time it took to finish a horn of mead. I wished then that he would go back to avoiding me."

Hakon's jaw muscles jumped.

"He told me later, on his death bed, that when I was born, he saw that the gods had marked me. The usual thing would be to get rid of me, as if I was a sick child. But my mother did not allow it, and he loved her too much to insist. They were both hoping to have more children, ones who would not be cursed. I remember much talk about it. Whispers. But nothing happened. Maybe he blamed me and my curse for it."

Hakon took another twig in his hands, snapped it, tossed it, and wrapped his arms around his knees. Mia felt the urge to reach out and comfort him. She knew all too well about strict, emotionally distant fathers. Where Hakon's mother had protected him, Mia's mother had just complied. What would her life be like if her mother had stood up to Mia's dad?

"And I only found out later, but that night, my father got an idea to send me on a trial. Alone in the woods, with just one ax. If I survived, I was not cursed. If I did not come back, the curse would have died with me. Either way, he wanted to get rid of the curse..." He choked on the last word. "Of me."

Mia wanted to cover his hand with hers but stopped. He did not want her pity. He wanted her to listen.

"But I did not know it that night," he continued, his voice emotionless. "It was so sudden. She woke me up and told me we needed to leave, just the two of us. All that was so strange, but I followed her. The look on my father's face when he stood at the gates. The sorrow, the fear, the goodbye..."

Hakon grimaced. "He did not stop us."

He glanced at Mia then, and there was raw pain in his eyes.

"So we went. The two of us and the horse. When we were in the middle of the woods, she said, 'We are going to my family, Hakon, and you will have to stay with them for a while. Until I can come get you. It is not safe at home for you anymore.'"

Mia's skin chilled.

"But we got lost," Hakon continued. "And in the middle of the woods, the wolves came."

Mia shook her head. "The wolves?"

"A pack. A dozen of them. The horse panicked. My mother told me to climb a tree and that she would follow. We would wait until we got help. So I started climbing. It was only when I was near the top that I realized she did not follow me."

Mia clutched her apron dress to her belly. "No...did they attack her?"

He bowed his head, and Mia closed her eyes, afraid of what he'd say next. "She knew if she stayed, we would both be dead.

She gave me a chance to survive. She led the pack away from me."

A tear crawled down Mia's face. She could see Dota and Hakon, a boy, but already a little man. Dota had done everything to save her son. Mia understood her very well. Cursed or not cursed, he was her child, and she was ready to cross a forest full of wolves to save him. To give her life for him...

Mia felt the same way about her baby.

"What happened then?" she said.

He looked up and reached to cup her jaw and gently swipe the tear away. Then he turned to the fire.

"I came down looking for her and saw the tracks in the snow. I realized what she had done and wanted to follow her. The pack was gone. But one wolf had stayed."

Mia's throat tightened.

"He was giant. Compared to a boy of twelve winters old, of course. I was under that pine, and he charged at me, full speed, flying through the snow. And something told me to roll to my side. It sounded like the wind. Maybe it was my mother. Maybe it was one of the gods who wanted to continue to torture me in this life. But I rolled. And the wolf landed in a small snowdrift under the tree. In the snowdrift was an old, dry stick as sharp as a spear. It pierced his neck. Then I finished him with the ax."

Mia's heart thumped as she saw the image in her head. Hakon, a twelve-year-old Viking with a bloody ax, a giant wolf at his feet, its blood darkening the snow around him.

"I followed the tracks then. They went far. Or maybe it just felt that way. I could not run fast enough. I thought my blood would turn to ice from fear for her."

He paused. His face went ashen, his eyes empty. Mia's hands covered her mouth.

"And then I found them. The horse and her. What was left of them. A part of me died then, when I saw her like that."

A chill ran over Mia's skin and her eyes burned from tears that now fell like raindrops. Her throat ached. "What did you do?"

"I carried her home. She deserved a ship burial. I could not leave her like that."

He threw another twig in the flames. In a few moments, it exploded, sending sparks into the darkening air.

"I arrived at the village around noon the next day. You should have seen their faces when I entered the mead hall with her frozen body in my arms. I had stopped feeling them long before from strain, from cold, but I would have rather died than let her go. Your father shot to his feet and touched Mjölnir, like everyone did."

Mia frowned. "King Nyr was there?"

"He was there. He was visiting. You know many of those who saw me at that moment. They would never forget that day. I swear to Odin, their first thought was that it was me who killed her."

Mia's heart bled. She understood now why the people were so afraid of Hakon. How could they be so superstitious?

"But they do not seriously believe a young boy would tear his mother apart like a wolf?" Mia said.

"When the shock passed, they did not think that anymore. But they became convinced it was my curse that caused her to die while I lived. They still believe that. They are afraid that is what I will do to them."

He glanced at her, anguish in his eyes.

"After the burial, I went to the woods and found that wolf. To never forget that I bring death to people who love me, I made this cloak out of his hide." He hooked the edge of the gray cloak he wore.

His eyes became amber in the orange light of the fire against the darkness. "That was the day I lost the person who I loved most in the whole of Midgard. Until I met you."

Mia could hear her own heart thumping, as if she was listening through a stethoscope.

"I never thought there was any future for me other than sorrow and destruction. But then you came. And you showed me that there's still hope for me. Maybe it's my mother who looked out for me from Fólkvangr, Freyja's field of the dead. I never wanted to fall in love with my wife."

Guilt pressed inside Mia's chest. She was lying to him, and he was in love with her. And he did not know about the baby, about the fact that she was from another time, or that after the epidemic was over and her patients no longer needed her she would be gone from his life forever.

The thought opened a sucking black hole in her chest. She had become so used to seeing him every waking second. She looked forward to working by his side in the hospital every morning, sleeping next to him at night. It was as if his very presence added to her joy, made her life worth living.

Imagining a life where he did not exist was like stabbing herself in the gut. Tears welled in her eyes, and pain hit her in the heart like a bullet.

Hakon must have seen the change in her face, because his eyes became worried. "I am not hurrying you to lie with me. You come to me when you are ready."

And now she was looking into the face of this man: his superhero birthmark, his short beard, his eyes the color of green amber, his blond hair framing his gorgeous face in soft curls.

The dearest face in all worlds... Love began thawing the ice in her heart and healing the parts of it that were torn. Just over two weeks had passed since Mia had met him. And she was feeling this?

Was she absolutely insane? She was a pregnant time traveler pretending to be someone else...

And yet, contrary to all logic and all rational thought, Mia was happier here with Hakon than she had ever been in her life.

What if she could stay here? What if she could really be his wife? She would need to tell him the truth, of course. But if he accepted her, how would she feel if she stayed? Waking up next to him every morning, feeling his hot, hard body covering hers.

And then the answer came—she would be truly happy.

Because she was falling in love with Hakon.

She refused to let herself think about all of the reasons she shouldn't stay. They could wait till tomorrow. For tonight, she would tell him the truth—the whole truth—and pray that he accepted her and understood.

But first...

She shifted towards him, her pulse racing, until she was kneeling next to him.

And very slowly, not nearly fast enough, her lips found his.

CHAPTER THIRTEEN

Hakon's lips were tender but firm. His beard tickled Mia's skin, adding to her excitement. His hands wrapped around her and he drew her to him, his body as hot as a stove.

Her blood pulsated with need. She arched into him, pressing herself against him. His body was rock-hard, his muscles unforgiving.

He parted her lips with his tongue, and she welcomed him, licking and sucking. He nipped at her lower lip gently, then cupped the back of her head and held it in place as his tongue dipped deeper into her mouth.

Mia's nipples hardened, her body began glowing with lust. He was tender but firm, slow but assertive.

His other hand slid down her spine to her ass, leaving a trail of liquid fire. He turned more fully towards her and pulled her hips until she straddled him.

Then he broke the kiss.

Mia was out of breath, delirious, trying to understand what was going on. His eyes darkened. He watched her with such longing that her breath caught in her throat.

"I want you, Arinborg," he growled. "I have since the moment I saw you. I swore I wouldn't touch you until you wanted me to." His voice, like a distant rumble, caressed her. "Do you want me to?"

Mia bit her lip, her body full of need. She'd sworn she wouldn't be vulnerable to another man. And she hadn't told him the truth about herself. In fact, it would be wisest to completely avoid any attraction.

Too late for that.

Her heart thumped, *Yes! Yes!* There was nothing that her body wanted more than to dissolve into him. And consequences be damned.

"Yes," she said, echoing her heart.

He growled, an animal sound. "Ah thank Freyja. I would need to go to the fjord to cool down should you have said no."

Mia chuckled, and before she could say something, his lips covered hers, his arms pinning her against him like a vise. Her hands slid up his hard chest and wrapped around his neck.

She longed for him—his warmth, his strength, his masculinity. She wrapped her legs around his waist, dragging herself close to him. His erection pressed against her crotch, and she moaned.

"I want you to moan like that when I'm inside you," he whispered against her mouth.

It was the sexiest thing she'd ever heard. Her skin covered with sweat, heat traveled through her bones.

One of his hands went to her breast and cupped it through her clothes. She gasped and arched into his touch. He circled her nipple with his thumb, and it hardened even more, sending jolts of pleasure through her.

"Gods, give me the strength not to tear off your clothes and throw myself at you," Hakon groaned, cupping both breasts.

She ran her fingers through his hair, desire flowing through her veins like liquid stardust.

He slid one big hand under her dress, then, and up her thigh. The hot, dry skin of his palm caressed and scratched her slightly. His hand traveled up her belly, and she froze for a moment, wondering if he'd notice the hardness of it, but he didn't.

Mia could tell he was controlling himself, doing his best to move slow, and his excitement thrilled her.

His hand slid higher still, until he reached her breast. Then the second hand followed, and he cupped them both, tugging and scraping her nipples until she could barely draw her breath.

"I want you naked," he said.

"I want you naked, too."

One corner of his lip curled up. "As you wish, Princess." He withdrew his hands and began undressing. Mia forgot everything watching him.

He removed the cloak, and with one swift motion drew his tunic up. Mia's breath caught as his naked body emerged, arms as thick as electric poles, pecs she could hike up, a six-pack that would make a bodybuilding champion weep. She just stared at him.

"Do you really exist?" she heard herself say.

She closed her mouth as his dark eyes watched her with predatory lust.

Then she threw herself on him, kissing him, and he fell onto his back. The skin of his chest felt smooth against the palm of her hand, the smattering of hair on his chest, crisp. She inhaled his musk, the scent of a man.

He rolled her over and pinned her to the ground. She wanted to feel him. She needed her skin to be sliding against his.

He undid the brooches, slid the apron dress down to her hips, then released the fastenings of the shift at the back of her neck. He made a low sound as he slid the shift down her shoulders—rough, impatient—but it only added to her excitement.

When she lay naked under him, he rose on one arm and looked her up and down without saying anything. Mia was sure no one had ever looked at her like that.

"You are a treasure sent to me by the gods. I have never seen a woman as beautiful as you. Are you truly mine?"

Tears burned in her eyes at his words.

"I am yours," she whispered.

He kissed her tears away, smiling, licking them off her face. Then dragged his lips down her neck towards her breasts, and she whimpered in anticipation.

He sucked one nipple, circled it with his tongue, and Mia gasped. He tugged at it gently with his teeth, scraping them across her taut flesh. Then he moved to the other breast and began going back and forth between them, nibbling and sucking.

"So pink. So delicious," he whispered, and her nipples began to ache.

He slid his hand down the curve of her waist.

"So thin. So beautiful."

And then down between her legs. He slid a thumb into her wetness, stroked it in circles and up and down. Mia rocked her hips, moaning as intense pleasure jolted through her in all directions.

"I have never desired a woman as I desire you," he whispered.

Mia spread her legs and hugged him. He rose to his knees, his torso gleaming slightly in the light of the fire. He began undoing his pants, his eyes on her, avid. Finally, his erection sprang free, and she licked her lips at the sight. He fisted his cock at the base, and the gesture was hot and carnal.

"Gods, I cannot wait any longer. I must have you," he said.

Mia ran her fingers down his hard pecs, his ripped stomach and stopped right before the curls surrounding his sex. "Have me," she whispered.

He positioned his erection against the swollen lips of her sex and caressed her with it as hot bliss traveled through her blood.

"I want to show you the stars," he said.

"Oh, I see them."

He found the center of her and continued his delicious torture until Mia couldn't take it anymore. She grabbed him by his waist, big and warm and hard, and urged him towards her.

"Take me," she said, looking into his eyes. "Now."

He licked his lips, lowered onto his elbows, and kissed her. Then he slid inside her, stretching her deliciously, filling her completely, and a deep moan escaped her throat. He withdrew slowly and glided back again gradually.

"Oh, you feel better than Valhalla," he whispered in her ear.

Mia spread her thighs even wider and urged him deeper, but he was still moving slowly in and out.

"I want you to savor this like the best feast of your life. The first of many to come."

He was teasing her, taking his time, stretching out the pleasure, and it was driving her wild. And she couldn't take it anymore. She felt he was holding back, but she needed him, needed more.

"Hakon, faster," Mia moaned. "I need you to be you. Let go."

"Argh!" he roared.

He began moving faster, harder, grunting and growling, and Mia thought she'd never heard anything hotter.

He continued thrusting into her, picking up speed. He grabbed a handful of her ass, making their body contact even fuller, adding a new, intense edge, and even more sweet pleasure.

Mia loved every moment, every thrust, every breath, every stroke, every groan.

He began to shudder, and she knew he was holding off to let her come first. And she was close.

The buildup was deep inside of her, and it took her, making her rise higher and higher, heating her up more and more.

Hakon shuddered, threw his head back, his muscles firm, still pounding inside of her, and shouting her fake name.

Mia convulsed in the sweetest of agonies as her release took her like a warm tempest, and her release surged against his.

When he collapsed on top of her and slid to her side, taking her into his giant, warm hug, Mia thought that she heard him whisper, "I love you." But she wasn't sure if it was only her raging heartbeat. A beat that answered, *I love you, too.*

Cold shiver ran through her, and she opened her eyes, her arms around Hakon. She stared into the night sky full of stars.

She loved Hakon. But he had just made love to Arinborg, the Norse princess. Not Mia, a pregnant runaway pediatrician from the future.

She should have told him the truth before they'd gone this far. The real Arinborg was out there somewhere, waiting to marry Hakon. And when she finally arrived, Mia would get her heart broken again. And so would Hakon.

She needed to tell him before that happened...even if it meant losing him.

CHAPTER FOURTEEN

HAKON DID NOT WANT to fall asleep. He could not.

If the gods had decided to forgive him, this was it. *She* was it.

He held Arinborg in his arms the whole night, her sweet breath tickling his chest, her hair spread on his shoulder and arm like a blanket. They were cuddled together under the cloaks, lying on the sheepskin. The fire died in the night, but Hakon did not stir to feed it. He was holding a gift far too precious to let go even for a moment.

He drifted off just before dawn.

Her movement woke him, her hair tickling his skin. She was sitting next to him, covering her breasts with the cloak, her silky hip pressed against his leg. The scent of her hair touched his nostrils. She smelled divine.

"Good morning." She smiled.

"A very good one."

The sun had risen and lit the ground next to them. Arinborg looked around, her eyes bright in wonder. The white mountain tops rested against the morning sky, their slopes dark green with the thick forest. Gentle wind rustled through the leaves. He loved that she was as much taken by this place as he was.

"Come here." Hakon tugged at her hand. She fell on his chest with a happy laugh, and he kissed her.

Her sweet smell enveloped him. Her soft lips and gentle tongue lit a wildfire in his veins, and he was instantly hard.

"Arinborg, I don't know if I ever can get enough of you," he whispered.

She stilled and leaned back, her eyes wide.

"What did I say?" Hakon said and sat up.

"No, no, nothing." She lowered her eyes and bit her lip. "It's me. I need to tell you something."

It was as if she had poured a bucket with freezing sea water over him. "What?"

She found her shift and put it over her head, still avoiding looking in his eyes. "I'll just feel better if I'm dressed when I tell you this."

Panic squeezed his gut like an iron fist. He had a sinking feeling that this was the end of his happiness.

No. He should not dive into the old habit of believing that he'd never be happy. What they had, what they'd said yesterday—

He stretched his hand out and lifted her chin gently with his finger. She met his gaze, and her green eyes were dark with welling tears.

"Arinborg, nothing you will say can break the bond between me and you, my wife."

She swallowed. "I'm pregnant."

Hakon frowned. He must have heard her wrong. "You are pregnant? Already? You cannot know that yet."

She tightened her hands into fists, then loosened them. "It's not yours. I was pregnant when I married you."

Rage rose up in his blood like the fountain of fire that scorched him from inside and the pain was excruciating. He jumped up, naked and all. "What?"

She looked up at him, her eyes big and full of sadness. "I'm sorry I didn't tell you before."

"You are sorry?" He felt as if she had stabbed him in the heart. He walked away from her and began pacing. He wanted to hit something.

The thought was rolling in his head like thunder: his wife was pregnant with another man's baby.

"I felt it in my bones that you were too good to be true. The gods do not want to grant me happiness. I could tell I was not your first, but I did not care. But this! Who is he?"

He stopped and glared at her. She was pale, still sitting on the sheepskins, clutching the fur cloaks that were wrapped around her legs. He wanted to kill the man in the most brutal way. Cut his balls off and throw them to the pigs.

"He—he is no one you know."

Hakon clenched his jaws. The next question made him go so rigid his whole body felt like cold stone. "Do you love him?"

"What? No! I don't. I thought I loved him once, but not anymore. We were," she paused, as if looking for a word carefully, "in a relationship."

What did it mean? Why was she using these strange terms?

"Were you married?"

"No. But we were close."

"Lovers?"

She looked down, as if in shame. "Yes."

"You were lovers, but unmarried."

The images of her body next to another man twisted his heart in agony.

"Why didn't you marry him? Did he seduce you?"

She met his gaze. "Our love died. He was the wrong man

for me. And when I wanted out, he—"

Her voice broke off and she looked down at her hands, and something about her hunched shoulders, her hands clasped together made his stomach feel as if a boulder had sunk in it.

"He wouldn't let me go."

"What do you mean? Did he hold you by force? Did he violate you?"

His fists clenched so hard they felt like they would never unclench. She was quiet for a long time.

"Answer me," he said.

She looked up at him, her face a bitter challenge. "Yes. Yes, Hakon." She rubbed her forehead with her hand, and it was shaking. "God, it's the first time I've told anyone."

His nostrils flared. "Did your father avenge you?"

She frowned. "No—"

He cut her off, too angry. "So your deceitful father married off his pregnant daughter to me, and did not even kill the man who took you against your will? He is even worse than I had thought."

Arinborg stood up now, alarm on her face. "He didn't know."

"You did not tell your father? Why not?"

She raised her chin. "I couldn't."

"Why?"

Arinborg hugged herself. "It's not something women are proud of, Hakon."

Hakon looked her up and down, then began putting on his pants. "You and your father," he scoffed. "You learned betrayal from him, did you not?"

"No! Hakon, I didn't mean—"

"Oh, you meant it. You knew and you hoped to marry a jarl instead of that man whoever he is, did you not?"

"But I am telling you now. After what you shared with me

yesterday, I couldn't live another day with the lie."

"How noble of you. And what do you want me to do now? Raise another man's child as my own?"

"I don't know. It's up to you, of course. But if you want me, you must accept my child."

The pain of her betrayal and deception, rage at the man who had hurt her, and jealousy were boiling and swirling and bubbling inside of him. He wanted to be the one who gave her a child.

"What is his name?"

"What?"

"His name. If your father did not avenge you, I will."

"How?"

"I will look for him when I—" he almost said, *burn your father's borg to the ground*, but cut himself off. He also had a secret from her that he had not shared yet, and guilt stung him. "When I visit your father. Tell me his name."

She hesitated but then nodded. "Dan."

He picked up his cloak and began rolling the sheepskin. He could not look at her. He was such a fool for believing for one moment that the gods favored him. It was the curse again. "Let us go back."

She laid her hand on his arm, but he withdrew without looking at her.

"Hakon, talk to me."

But he only went on packing.

"What happened to 'nothing can break the bond between us'?" she asked, her voice shaking.

He clenched his jaw. One part of him wanted to take her in his arms. But that was a very small part. His beast thundered inside of him from anger and pain and loneliness.

"Odin help me, you deceived me! I need to think, woman. You would be wise to stay out of my way."

CHAPTER FIFTEEN

During the next three days Hakon didn't guard Mia, nor did he sleep in their bedroom.

Their bedroom... She was so silly thinking of it as *their* bedroom! Wasn't this exactly what she had wanted to avoid—falling for a guy and calling things *theirs*? She barely knew him. She had rushed into a relationship with Dan, thinking she had fallen in love with him, and moved in too quickly. And look where it had gotten her.

No more.

But Hakon's withdrawal hurt.

Not only had he avoided her, he'd barely said a word to her since they'd returned from the mountain. The night they were there had felt like a small honeymoon.

But it was just an illusion, to think that everything would be all right, that she would be a Viking's wife. She was an idiot.

How could she have thought she could stay here at all? Was she insane? Give birth here? Raise her child here? She was making that mistake again, following her emotions rather than thinking clearly.

She had hidden so much from him, and now he didn't even care anymore if she ran away or stayed.

Well, at least she was still safe. If he had reacted like that about the pregnancy, what would he have done if she had told him the whole truth—that she was not princess Arinborg at all? What would the people of the village do?

They would probably throw her out, wouldn't they? It was hard to imagine that they would actually harm her, or that Hakon would let them. But, in any case, Mia was safer under her fake identity.

At least for today.

Mia and Hakon had not seen each other much during the day, Mia being busy at the hospital. And Hakon... Well, who knew where he was? When they saw each other at dinner and she sat in her chair by his side, she felt his careful sideways glances on her skin like pin pricks. But when she looked back at him, he was staring at his bowl and brooding.

She tried several times to talk to him, but he only demanded that she leave him alone. Mia had a hard time falling asleep without him by her side. Jealousy clawed at her heart. What if he was looking for comfort in the arms of another woman, like Dan had? Every morning, he came to breakfast in disarray, hay in his hair and his clothes rumpled.

On the breakfast of the fourth day, Mia demanded to know where he had been, her voice shaking.

He blurted, "I slept in the slaves' shed."

Relief flooded her. Slaves and servants all shared a house that was full of hay for them to sleep. It had barely any walls, let alone any privacy with a dozen or so people there.

"When will you come back?" she said, damn pregnancy hormones swirling her relief and intensifying it into a tornado, her eyes blurring.

He turned away from her, took a spoonful of his oats, chewed, then said, "I have not decided."

"Let me know when you do. I miss you," she whispered and left the great hall to go to the hospital.

The next day, when Mia was listening to the chest of a ten-year-old boy with a hearing tube that she had asked the carpenter to make, Oda's voice rang through the hospital. "Mistress! Princess Arinborg! Mette is choking!"

Mia rushed to Oda, who was cradling the little bundle with Mette. Ever since Mia and Hakon had come back from the mountain, Mette had gotten progressively worse. Her airways were closing tighter every day, and the episodes when she could not get air in between coughing fits were longer.

One glance told her Mette was choking. Her little lips were blue, her face turning purple, the skin around her eyes red from strain, and her little hands grabbing at empty air. Mia felt all the blood drain from her face and neck, her hands and feet turning to ice.

"Oh my god! I need a suction tube!" She looked around hopelessly for a moment. She'd been trying to figure out a suitable solution for the past three weeks, but the sad fact was that she needed something plastic. Nothing in the Viking Age would work. But she didn't have anything except the contents of her purse, which were mostly useless. Why didn't she have a first aid kit in there, at least, instead of such silly things as a glow-in-the-dark bracelet?

The answer she'd been searching for flashed into her mind like a light in the darkness. If she emptied the fluid it just might work... "We have to run, can you run, Oda?"

Mia was already tugging the woman, and they flew.

Under normal circumstances, it was probably a two-minute walk to the great hall. If they ran, they might cover it in half a minute. Mette might have a minute until she became dangerously deprived of oxygen. Mia would have no time to check if the suction tube worked before she used it on Mette.

It had to work.

If not, this would be the first death on Mia's hands.

People, houses flashed by as Mia and Oda ran, Mia tugging the woman after herself because she was slower with the baby in her arms.

"Arinborg!" she heard Hakon's voice calling after her.

It was the first time he'd addressed her directly since her confession.

"Not now, Hakon!"

They ran through the mead hall, right into the bedchamber. Her back to Oda, Mia went through her purse and grabbed the glow-in-the-dark bracelet. She twisted off the top and emptied the liquid onto the floor, then whisked the tube through a bucket of fresh water. Mette's eyes were bulging now, panic in them, her lips blue. She had little time before her little brain would become completely deprived of oxygen and she would die. Mia opened Mette's mouth and carefully inserted one end into her throat. The baby gagged a little. Mia put the other end of the tube into her own mouth.

And sucked the air in.

Mucus came, and she spat it out. She sucked again, and more mucus came. Mette still couldn't breathe.

It must be an airway spasm. Mia needed to do mouth-to-mouth resuscitation and push the air past the spasm. She took Mette from Oda, the baby tense and hard in her arms, and put her flat on the bed. Mia pressed her lips to the baby's mouth and carefully blew. She had to be very cautious not to blow in too much air as Mette's lungs were much smaller than her own.

Finally, Mette breathed in, making that whooping sound that had become too familiar, a sound that meant bad news—

but in this instance, it brought relief.

She breathed in more and cried, then more whooping and another cry. Oda grabbed her in her arms, and pressed the girl to herself, sobbing with joy.

A shadow appeared next to Mia, and Hakon's hands were on her shoulders, massaging her.

His hands, heavy and warm, finally brought her back to her senses. She turned into his arms, into his bear hug. His scent of hay, musk, and slightly tired clothing enveloped her. She pressed her face into his chest and cried soundlessly, relieved that Mette had lived, that the bracelet had worked, and that Hakon was there like a safe haven.

His arms wrapped around her, soothing, stroking her, warming her up, and Mia calmed down. She had saved the baby. She looked up at Hakon without breaking the hug, and he watched her, his golden-green eyes tender.

"Are you all right?" Mia said.

His eyebrows rose. "You are asking me if I am all right? Now?"

"I've barely seen you for four days, and you aren't talking to me. I want to know how you are."

He smiled. "Better now."

Mia smiled back. She wanted to kiss him so bad. She missed his hard, warm body, and she wanted to get him naked and feel his skin against hers.

Hakon looked at the bed where the bracelet lay. "What is that?"

Mia's heart pounded against her ribs. She swallowed hard. "A healer gave it to me, back home. I'm not sure what it's made of. But does it matter? It saved Mette."

Hakon studied her, then gave a nod. Mia hid her face against his chest, guilt heavy in her heart. He trusted her. He believed her without question. What would happen once he found out?

She almost jumped as a suckling noise reached her—she had forgotten for a moment that they were not alone. She turned back, and sure enough, Mette was breastfeeding, smacking her lips in delight.

"You." Mia heard Oda's low voice and turned around. The woman's face was livid, and she was glaring at Hakon. "It is you and your curse. Because of you my daughter almost died. You held her! You cursed her! Your bad luck brings death to everyone around you."

Mia broke contact with Hakon and shielded him from her. "Oda, calm down. It is not a curse—"

"What else? All other children are the same or getting better. Only my daughter almost suffocated. Because he cursed her."

"He did not. There is no curse. She was just a little unlucky, but we saved her."

"Everyone should know about this. We need to do something before he brings another misery on us."

Mia noticed Hakon had crossed his arms over his chest, his eyebrows bunched together.

Nothing Mia could say would convince Oda otherwise. So Mia had to play by her rules. "All right," Mia said. "All right. You think he's cursed? I will remove his curse."

Oda frowned. "You?"

"Yes, me. I'm a healer."

Mia had realized in the time she'd been here that in Viking culture, mysticism and medicine were considered one. Healers were shamans, like Solveig. People must think Mia was the same.

She continued, "I can remove curses just like I can heal

wounds and diseases. Wouldn't you agree that this would be wise?"

Oda studied her, then her face brightened. "That would be wise."

"Good then." Mia winked at Hakon and went to her purse. The Tylenol bottle was there. She had given some in powder form to children with high fever, without anyone seeing what she was doing. But this time, she wanted them to watch.

There was only one pill left, and she removed it from the bottle without Hakon and Oda seeing. She showed the pill to them, bringing it directly to their eyes.

Then she went into the great hall and found a pestle and a soapstone bowl for grinding herbs and took a cup with water. She brought them to the bedchamber and put the pill into the bowl. They watched with wide eyes, full of curiosity and wonder. She then took the pestle and started grinding the pill into powder, closed her eyes and began humming "Thriller" by Michael Jackson and swaying as if in a trance.

When she felt that the pill was fully ground, she opened her eyes, wriggled her fingers over the bowl and said, "Curse, begone!"

She then poured half a mug of clean water into the bowl and stirred it. It was a pity to use the last painkiller she had, but it would be worth it if Oda believed her. She would tell everyone else in the village.

Mia took the bowl with both hands and held it out to Hakon. "Curse, begone!" she said again and made him drink.

He frowned, bulged his eyes, but like an obedient patient, drank.

When the bowl was empty and Mia removed it from his lips, he grimaced in disgust. "What was that? Bird's shit?"

"Bitter, huh?" Mia said, then shrugged. "Better that you don't know."

Oda watched him carefully, Mette sleeping peacefully in her arms. "Well?" Oda said.

"What?" Mia asked.

"How are you feeling, Hakon?"

Hakon blinked. "Like a new man."

CHAPTER SIXTEEN

Oda and Mette finally left the room, and Hakon was alone with his princess.

The medicine she had given him was still bitter on his tongue, and he had never tasted anything so foul, but he was ready to drink anything out of her hands. She had told him he was not cursed, planting a seed of doubt in him about that, but when Mette had almost died, he'd known Arinborg was wrong.

But she had saved the baby's life. Because she was the healer. She was the blessing.

And she had healed him. He knew that.

The dull headache he had had since this morning, from drinking himself to sleep with mead, was fading away. Pain from an old wound on his hip that bothered him after he slept on the ground weakened.

Arinborg was so beautiful he could not breathe. Her eyes bright and shiny, her lips pink and inviting, a healthy blush on her cheeks. Her hair was done in braids on her head but left streaming down her shoulders and back. He could not believe this woman was his.

He had spent the past four days without her, longing for her. Once he had experienced the taste of her body, of plunging into her depths, of making her his, he had known he would never get enough of her. The nights spent without her were a torture.

Fear gripped his gut. The fear of losing her. Fear of the gods, who could still take her away. She was too good to be true.

Yes, she was with another man's child, which she had concealed from him. Hakon clenched his jaws as the thought called his anger back to the surface.

Arinborg raised her brows. "Are you ready to talk now?"

"What is there to talk about?"

"Well, you said you needed time to process the news. Did you have enough time?"

"I do not know if there will ever be enough time, Arinborg."

She hugged her waist, her eyes watering.

"What should we do then? Should I go? Is that what you want?"

The thought of her leaving felt like the slash of a sword against his core. "I do not know. It seemed like that is what you wanted when you first arrived."

"I can't leave yet, not when people are still sick." Her voice was barely audible.

Hakon was torn between relief and pain. "Is that the only reason?"

"You tell me. Will you accept my baby?"

Accepting another man's child—he could not even accept the notion of being a father himself.

Not after how his father was with him. He did not know how to be a good father. He did not know how to be a good husband. All he knew was how to be a good warrior.

And the Beast.

Was he still the Beast after that bitter potion? Was he the Beast after the curse was lifted?

"I want you to stay my wife."

With two steps he crossed the distance between them and cupped her face with both hands. "And I need to make love to you in our bed."

"What about—"

He kissed the rest of her words away.

He did not know yet if he was ready to accept another man's child, but he knew that he was not ready to let her go, and he had to feel her in his arms. The small glimpse of happiness that she had given him was like the best mead he had ever tasted.

He wanted more.

Her lips were soft, and her mouth was warm, wet, and luscious. She moaned against him, and the sound echoed through his whole body to the end of his cock. Her tongue met his and probed his mouth, sending bolts of pleasure through his veins.

"Did you miss me?" he growled as he dragged his lips down her neck, tasting her skin like a man after a week of hunger.

"Like crazy." The words came out as a needy sigh, and her fingers dug into his shoulder blades.

The sensation was on the verge of pain and pleasure, the perfect mirror of what he had been feeling ever since he had met her, and it made thunder vibrate in his bones.

He inhaled her scent, as if he had been suffocating and she was a gust of fresh air. Undoing her brooches, he let the apron dress fall to the floor. Then her shift followed.

He took a small step back, holding her hands so that she did not get any ideas of covering herself. Then he took his pleasure looking her over. Up on the mountain, he had never gotten a chance to really see her.

And now...

She stood with her chin up. She wanted him to like her, he could tell.

If she only knew that he would have loved her even if she had the body of a troll.

But she looked like the goddess Freyja herself. Her neck delicate, her skin glowing like mother-of-pearl, her breasts round, as if destined to perfectly fit his hands. Her narrow waist with the swell of her belly down where her child was growing inside of her, going into the round hips and the triangle of soft curls, the sight of which made his cock jerk. Her long legs, he wanted to kiss every little bit of them.

"You are so beautiful," he heard himself whisper. "The elves must have made you out of sea foam and spring flowers."

She sniffled softly. "They didn't. Trust me. Your turn, mister."

He chuckled. "Do you want me to undress?"

"Very much."

Hakon swallowed, still not sure if he was pleasing for her to look at. He was big, yes, but did she like what she saw? Was he not too much like the Beast?

But he obliged without hesitation. First came the tunic, then the pants.

When he straightened and looked at her, she was regarding him with burning eyes.

"Am I not disgusting to you?" he asked.

Her eyes widened. "If I hear a single word about the curse, I swear, Hakon, I will throw something at you. And you better pray it's not one of your axes."

He breathed a little easier, but she must have seen something in his face, because then her eyes turned soft. She took a step closer and pressed her silky warm body against him, and he wrapped his arms around her small frame.

"Hakon"—she laid her palms on his chest, burning him—"you are the most attractive man I have ever seen. You are not just gorgeous, you are unforgettable. Your body is every woman's dream."

What strange words for a woman to say, as if she had seen so many men's bodies, as if she knew what other women dreamed of in a man. She was a healer, a witch, and a princess—he still struggled to understand the depths of her.

"You do like how I look?" he said.

"I *love* how you look, Hakon," she whispered. "Now shut up and make love to me."

"As you wish, my blessing."

He kissed her, hardening with every pull of the lips, every stroke of the tongue, her luscious taste as fresh as a high mountain spring.

He moved down, pressing his lips against her neck, feeling the violent beat of her vein under his tongue. When he reached her breasts, he licked one nipple, then sucked, and it felt firm and petal-soft in his mouth. She moaned, her fingers running through his hair and digging into his scalp. She smelled like life—maybe it was the pregnancy or just her. The healer. Life-giver. His blessing.

His.

Hakon continued his exploration, worshiping her body, the silk of her skin, the narrowness of her waist. And then he came to the firm swell of her lower belly and froze. He put his hand on it and heard her hold her breath. The baby was part of her. And if she was his, then it was also his.

If it was another man's that did not matter.

If it was hers, it was Hakon's.

He gently kissed her belly, and caressed it with his hand, and heard her breathe again.

Then he went even further down, to the aim of his

exploration.

The curls of her hair down there. He dipped his finger in her warm, soft, silky folds, and she gasped. He slowly slid his finger up and down her folds until she moaned and pressed her fingers deeper into his hair.

That was the center of her pleasure. He began rubbing, circling, and her moans intensified, her thighs shaking.

Good.

He withdrew his hand and kissed her there instead. His tongue dipped into the silkiness of her folds and began probing her there, licking, teasing, playing. She moaned and trembled and shook and got even wetter.

"Oh, Hakon, I can't stand," she moaned, and he straightened, grabbed two handfuls of her round ass and lifted her up. Her legs wrapped around his waist.

"Then I will hold you," he said.

His cock was right at her sleek entrance, her eyes were locked with his, her breasts squished against him.

He slid into her, feeling as if he had just come home after a long raiding season, and she gasped, arching into him, her head falling back. Her insides were tight and sleek and hot, and liquid pleasure spilled through Hakon.

He moved slowly at first, savoring, letting her get used to him, making sure she enjoyed the ride. Her cries were like tar to fire, making him burn like never before.

Her skin covered in sweat, she met his thrusts with her own movements.

And soon—too soon, and not soon enough—he was close, and he felt her body tense, too.

And with a few more strong thrusts, she was trembling all around him, milking him, caressing him. He was riding the waves of a storm of pleasure, and she was the sea goddess that had called it forth.

CHAPTER SEVENTEEN

MIA STROKED A THIN, silver scar on Hakon's chest. She was sinking in the deliciousness of his strong body, his arms around her, his shoulder under her cheek, his even breath tickling her skin. The semidarkness of their bedroom was peaceful and calming, the fire in the hearth cozy. The room smelled of sex, wood, and leather.

She could get used to this. Waking up every day to him, treating people here, helping Hakon with feasts, cooking, and overseeing the harvest. She could even learn to knit, weave, and sew, something women here were responsible for. And her baby...could she really imagine her son growing up in the Viking Age?

She didn't know.

She was sure she and her child would be safe with Hakon, as much as it was possible. But neither she nor Hakon would have any control over the diseases that might come. She had no way of producing antibiotics, no laboratory, not even a scalpel in case she needed to perform a surgery. Maybe she could make ethanol with time to disinfect wounds and such, but there were so many kinds of wounds that were life-threatening here.

No wonder people believed in gods, curses, and magic.

Maybe she could travel back and forth in time. Then she would have access to modern medicine and could bring the drugs and tools she would need here to help people even more.

But if she traveled back in time to Boston, would she be able to return to the Viking Age? What if she couldn't?

The thought chilled her to the bone, and she shivered. Hakon pulled her tighter to him.

"Are you cold, Arinborg?"

Arinborg…

Mia, she wanted to correct him, but bit her tongue.

She still needed to tell him that secret.

But not now.

She still didn't even know how he felt about her pregnancy.

"I was afraid you would send me away if you knew I was pregnant. Back to…him. To Dan. I am still afraid you will."

He rubbed her arm with his hand, and delicious heat spread through her. She moaned in bliss. Then his hand ran down her arm slower, and Mia held her breath. It landed on her belly and stroked it gently.

Mia looked up at him, and his yellow-green eyes were full of tenderness.

"I will not let that man breathe the same air as you," he said. "He will never touch a hair on your head again. I will take your child as my own."

She covered his hand with hers. "Really?"

He gave a curt nod, his eyes intense.

And then something happened. She had felt small flutters, like butterfly wings in her stomach more and more over the course of the past couple of weeks, but now there was a proper movement, as if a warm fish turned in her belly. Mia and Hakon both froze.

"Did you feel that?" Mia whispered.

"I did."

Delight spread in her body like a wave of giggles. She squeezed his hand. "I think it's a sign. The baby wants you, too."

He pressed his lips to her forehead. "It is. I will not be the kind of father to this child that my own father was to me. It was not your fault that you were violated, and it was not this child's fault that the person who gave it life is a disgrace of a man. Just like it was not my fault that I was born with the mark of a beast. I know how it feels to be unwanted. And I will not let you or this child ever feel that."

Mia's heart was thumping so fast, it felt like it would burst —of gratitude, of healing, of tenderness for this man.

Of love.

"I love you, Hakon," she whispered.

He closed his eyes as if to take a moment and recuperate from a blow. Then he opened them, and they were bright and light and shiny. "As I love you, Arinborg."

That name again, it hit her like a sledgehammer.

She should tell him.

Now.

"I am still afraid that something will go wrong," he said. "Death does not frighten me as much as the thought that the gods have given you and your love to me only to take this happiness away."

Mia's heart squeezed. He had no idea how right he was. Better tell him now. Then there would be no more lies standing between them.

God, what had happened to the real Arinborg? Was she

even alive? Even if something had happened to her, surely King Nyr would eventually want to see his daughter.

"And if they do take you away," he said. "I do not know if I can survive that."

Her stomach turned into a rock.

Tell him, now! I am not Arinborg. My name is Mia and I'm a time traveler from the future.

She opened her mouth, but nothing came out. She just couldn't bear to change the happiness on his face to pain. He would probably think she was crazy anyway. And even if he believed her, she could not be the one who gave him the news that the gods had exactly that in mind. It would only confirm in his mind that he was the beast everyone believed him to be.

Later. She would prepare him, in time. She would give him gentle signs. She would soften the blow.

"I'll heal you then," she said and kissed him. "I won't let the gods do anything to you."

CHAPTER EIGHTEEN

Days flew by like a happy dream.

The disease was coming to an end. A moon and a week passed, and one hospital was free of the sick, and went back to being a house. Thanks to his wife's skills, no one died. People were returning to their daily activities, and they were even warming up to him.

It was all Arinborg.

His wife.

His love.

She had promised to not let the gods take away their happiness. But she might not want to keep that promise by the end of summer.

Because he was still going to kill her father. He was still waiting for his allies. And he still could not tell her. He had discussed the plan with his loyal men, and they would not tell even their wives, so bound were they by their word to Hakon.

The preparations for the feast were going well. Mead was brewing. There was enough rye for bread and vegetables for stew. Servants and thralls were all almost back to good health and he knew there was enough manpower to prepare the feast when the jarls arrived.

His wife's belly swelled more and more, and she was getting more and more beautiful every day. So beautiful, he stopped breathing for a moment every time he glanced at her.

With more free time away from the hospital, she became more involved in the household chores. The great house was cleaner, and the food tasted better. Their bed was fresher. She liked to bathe every day, and the thralls were used to heating up the bathhouse for her. She had discussed with him the repairs of the houses and sheds, and he had given her full control. He just had not thought that the houses needed to be repaired; he had thought they would keep till later, with the revenge and raids on his mind.

Arinborg made everything better.

And the people loved her. Hakon saw her going to gather herbs with Oda and other women, cooking with them—even though as the jarl's wife, she did not have to do that. She sewed a gown for the baby. Another woman lent her a crib, and it already stood in the bedchamber.

When the watchman finally sounded the arrival of the first longship one week later, Hakon was filled with both anticipation and dread. The purpose of his entire life— avenging his mother's death—was within his reach. But he was lying to his wife, and very likely destroying his only chance at happiness.

It was Jarl Vefuss—Hakon recognized his white-and-red sails as soon as they were visible. Hakon and his wife waited on the wooden pier, ready to welcome their guests.

Jarl Vefuss was a man in his fifties, his beard and hair already white, but his might still obvious. He brought his two sons, tall and proud and seemingly good warriors. He came with fifty men.

The next day, Jarl Brunn arrived with another fifty, and the day after, Jarl Rafr with thirty more.

The village was swarming with people, and Arinborg and he were busy entertaining guests.

The night of the day Jarl Rafr arrived, they started the feast, and Hakon needed to discuss the matter of Nyr in private with the jarls. The three jarls watched Arinborg with respect but caution, knowing that she was their enemy's daughter. Surprisingly, none of them had seen her before. Hakon supposed it was understandable that they would not know her given that Nyr had nine daughters, but he could not imagine how any man could overlook a woman like her.

The feast was fully underway, the mead hall loud with laughter and the hum of voices, rich with the scents of roasted boar, cooked vegetables, and freshly baked bread. Mead flowed like a river. And Arinborg was so beautiful, Hakon's heart stopped every time he looked at her.

The doors to the great hall flew open. "Where is Hakon the Beast?" roared a woman he had never seen before.

The hall went quiet.

"Here," he said, standing up.

"Is this how you meet your bride?" she shouted. "You do not send a greeting party? You do not worry where she is?"

Hakon frowned, confused. The woman had long dark hair, a rich woolen cloak trimmed with fur, and a beautiful blood-red dress. She was quite lovely, but possibly insane.

"My bride is right here." He gestured at Arinborg, who stood up as well, pale. "And who are you?"

The woman's dark eyes threw lightning bolts into his wife, and he shifted instinctively to protect her.

"I am Princess Arinborg Nyrdotje. Your wife-to-be. I was delayed because I received an injury on my journey. And who is *she*?"

Chapter Nineteen

Mia had lied to them all. And now they knew it.

Her world was collapsing in the dim light of the great hall. Everyone stared at her. The faces of men and women she'd come to love, working every day side by side to fight the epidemic, or curing them or their children.

And yet, their opinion didn't matter as much as one person's.

Hakon glared at her with such intensity that she wanted to hide somewhere. One part of his face—the dark side with the birthmark—was in the light, and the other part in the shadows. It was as if the predator, the wolf in him, had taken over.

Mia shuddered.

"What is she talking about?" he said, his voice harsh and grating.

She had known this would happen eventually. This stupid plan had never had a happy ending. She should have told him a long time ago.

"She is the real Princess Arinborg," she said.

People around the room gasped.

Hakon grimaced as if she'd physically wounded him and looked her up and down, as if seeing her for the first time.

"Hakon," began Jarl Brunn, who sat by Hakon's other side, "if she is not the princess, King Nyr—"

"Not now. I need to talk to my wife." He offered Mia his hand. "Come."

His voice was soft, but it had a steel edge to it. Mia rose on legs as weak as cooked spaghetti, pins and needles in her arms and feet. But she held her head high and straightened her back. This might be the end of her and Hakon, and that would be her fault. But it was her chance to explain everything to him and hope that he would forgive her again.

Forgive yet another betrayal.

He led her outside. Even though it was evening, there was still a lot of light. The sun was just beginning to sink behind the mountain, setting the water of the fjord ablaze with red and orange. The wind rustled, evening crickets began their chirping, and the air smelled of flowers and grass. Hakon led her to the beach where no one would hear them.

When they came to the rocky shore, water splashing under their feet, Mia's heart was thumping so hard, it threatened to jump out of her chest. She was sweaty and hot, and she sank to her knees, leaned over the water and splashed it into her face. It was slightly salty, cool, and smelled of the sea, and it washed some of her anxiety away.

Hakon studied her, his face a stone mask. She knew it was a cage that held his real feelings inside under lock and key. But his eyes were free. They were dark, and there was fury in them, and pain, and questions.

"Talk," he said.

Mia closed her eyes for a moment, considering if there was a way to say things in some sort of order that would make sense and soften the blow. But she couldn't see it.

"My name is Mia Lindsay. I am from the future."

He blinked. "Are you taking me for a fool?"

"I know it sounds crazy. I was born in 1993 in San Diego, United States of America. That probably doesn't make much sense to you because it's the Christian calendar, and America is not even colonized yet. Anyway, I come from about eleven hundred years in the future. I am a doctor—well, almost. I had to stop my residency because of Dan, the man I told you about. The white powder I gave you is a painkiller. A pill I had with me when I traveled back in time."

She began talking faster and faster, trying to find the arguments quickly to persuade him, before he could cut her off and she'd lose her chance.

"The suction tube was a plastic bracelet I had with me. All those strange words that you are always asking me about...the fork...bathing...my dress with the flower print...my purse... All of the questions I asked about things that seemed obvious to you...common knowledge."

He closed his eyes for a moment and shook his head. "You are a strange one. You come up with such nonsense and want me to believe this?"

"I do!"

His lips tightened into a thin, angry line in his beard, then he took a step and grabbed her by the arm, shaking her slightly. Mia shrank at first, surprised, but then straightened her shoulders.

"You have been lying to me about everything that you are. Everything! Your name, where you are from. You didn't tell me a true thing about yourself. I have been living with a woman who does not exist. I have been falling in love with a woman that is an illusion."

His words squeezed and twisted her stomach, the pain excruciating.

"Tell me the truth, *Mia*," he continued, "or whoever you are. Why did you come here? Why did you pretend to be someone you are not?"

Mia clenched her jaw. "I didn't have a choice. You just grabbed me, put me on your horse, and threatened me with death if I wasn't Princess Arinborg. So I had to be her. Then I was looking for an escape, until the epidemic started. I couldn't leave until I made sure everyone got through it. And then—"

She swallowed. The knot in her throat hurt. His eyes, his mouth, were right in front of her. She itched to trace his eyebrow, the one on the side of the birthmark. It was bright blond against the darker skin.

"And then I fell in love with you."

He let go of her and took a step back, grimacing as if he was about to spit. "I do not believe a word. If you really loved me, you would have told me the truth."

Pain stabbed Mia in the heart. He was right. This was exactly what she was afraid of.

"I wanted to. I almost did. But I couldn't bear to see you brokenhearted. To see you like this."

He shook his head. "I knew the gods would not let me be happy. It was the curse all along."

Her stomach dropped.

"I lied because I was afraid of you in the beginning. I had to do anything to protect my baby. Anything. Like any mother would."

His face went blank at that, the anger gone. Ah yes, he knew that all too well, and he knew she was right. He was listening now, and hope flickered in Mia.

"After Dan..." she continued. "His name is Dan Pavarotti. He is a mafia lord in Boston, which means he has a huge criminal organization under him. Three years ago, we started dating. I had no idea he was a criminal back then, or I never would have become involved with him..."

And then she told him everything. Words poured out of her like pus from a wound. For the first time since she had met him, she was talking about her real self.

And it felt good.

She told him things she had never told anyone. How her father had always controlled her mom and her. How she had found another control freak in Dan. How in the beginning he was every woman's dream. He'd courted her, spoiled her, showered her with attention, and even named a yacht after her. How he'd begun beating her because he didn't know how else to keep her by his side. How she'd tried to escape him twice, and how his men had always found her and returned her to him. How he'd raped her after the second escape attempt, and she'd gotten pregnant. They hadn't been intimate for a while by then, and Dan had been caught in a rage and hadn't used a condom. How she'd found the strength to convince him to end an unhappy relationship for both of them. And how he'd found out that she was carrying his child the day before she could disappear forever.

And how that old lady had given her a golden spindle in the hospital so that she could escape. How the next thing Mia knew she was surrounded by the woods, the rock with the runes standing by her side, and a roaring bear charging her.

And Hakon.

He frowned. "A golden spindle?"

"Yes. Why?"

"Only a Norn would have a golden spindle."

"A Norn?"

"Norns spin people's fates." He studied her, then rubbed his forehead. "This tale you told me— It is very hard to believe. But if it is true, a Norn sent you here. And the rune stone in the sacred grove must have been why you appeared there. That is where we do sacrifices and praise the gods. There is a lot of magic in that place."

Mia inhaled deeply and nodded. Her instinct to go to the rune stone had been right.

Their eyes locked. "So you are not his daughter."

"Whose? King Nyr's?"

He laughed bitterly. "I don't know if I am relieved or concerned. If I am not married to Arinborg, the work of the past years to avenge the death of my mother has just perished."

Mia frowned. "Avenge the death of your mother?"

He turned away and walked a few steps, then turned back to her, his hands on his hips. Mia waited for the answer as if her life depended on it. The sun sank even lower behind the mountain, spilling flamingo-pink, red, and orange across the skies, turning into blue, and then almost black on the other side.

"When my father was dying, he told me what really happened that night. Nyr gave him the idea to test my curse."

She had a feeling she didn't want to know the answer, but she had to ask anyway. "So why did you want to marry his daughter?"

"Because I am going to kill him by the end of this summer, with the help of Jarl Brunn, Jarl Rafr, and Jarl Vefuss."

The ground sank under Mia's feet. "What?"

"This marriage was supposed to distract him. He wanted me on his side to fight his wars for him. He got me. He wouldn't know what had struck him until we'd attacked. But now that everyone knows that you are not Arinborg, I have no chance. The other jarls will fear catching Nyr's attention before we can act."

Mia swallowed. "If you have no more chance, there's no need to get revenge anymore, right?"

"No need to get revenge? I will never stop hunting him until I avenge my mother's death."

"So you hid from Arinborg—or me—that you were going to kill her father."

He nodded.

Something dark turned in Mia's stomach. Something she had not felt since she'd found out what Dan really did for a living.

Realization that she'd fallen in love with the image of a man, again, rather than seeing his true nature, slammed the air from her chest. Fear chilled her to the bone. The reality of that man was terrifying.

A man who was ready to kill the father of the wife he supposedly loved.

She stopped breathing. "And you are blaming *me* for lying? I lied to save my baby! You are lying to kill the father of your wife!"

Hakon took a step towards her. "Lower your voice!"

Mia breathed heavily and hugged herself, seeing him in a completely different light now. "How could I be so stupid? I thought I'd finally found the man for me. Even though I swore to myself I wouldn't rush into relationships, I would first gain independence and take care of my baby. And yet what have I done? Fallen in love with a Viking from eleven hundred years ago! A Viking who would put a blood feud above his love."

Hakon scowled at her. "But he is not *your* father. Why do you care?"

"Why do I care? I care because the man I thought I'd fallen in love with doesn't exist. I thought you were noble and kind and good-hearted. Turns out, you are a cold-blooded killer. I have already run from one so that my baby wouldn't be raised by such a man. And I won't let another one raise him, either."

Panic flickered in his eyes. He took a step towards her. "What are you saying?"

"I'm leaving. What was I thinking, imagining that I could stay in the past with you, give birth here, raise my son here? With *you*? I was ready to forget vaccination, modern hospitals, and the lack of proper education. But I can't be in a relationship with a man whose sole purpose in life is revenge."

He clenched his fists. "It is the destiny of Hakon the Beast."

Tears burned her eyes. "You are drinking the poison of revenge, and you don't even realize that you are the one dying. Stop, Hakon. Nyr already killed your mother. Don't let him kill you."

He looked like a hurt animal. She wanted to reach out and soothe him. But there was no future for them. Not after this.

"Goodbye, Hakon. Tell everyone I am sorry," she whispered. Then she turned away and walked towards the sacred grove.

She thought she saw him lifting up one hand as if to grasp her, but she must have imagined it.

She could only hope the rune rock would take her back, and once she was in Boston, that Dan had forgotten about her.

But she would never forget Hakon.

CHAPTER TWENTY

"Forgive me, lord, but you are not listening," Arinborg's voice dragged Hakon out of his daydream, in which the woman with a delicate swollen belly, hair the color of new honey, and eyes like the first grass of the year, was telling him that she loved him.

The day was gray, and rain drizzled on the village in a fine mist, the air thick with the smell of wet wood and earth. It was cold despite the summer season, steam rushing out of people's mouths as they stood and watched the fjord where a longship was approaching.

A longship bearing King Nyr's colors.

A week had passed since Mia left, the days dragging like he was living on the bottom of a swamp. Hakon was split between the pain of her betrayal, which tore his heart like a mace with sharp nails, and worry for her that sent his head spinning. If that man, Dan, found her... Hakon's fists clenched.

But he could not do anything about that. She'd left; she did not see a future with him. And he did not, either. It was for the best. He had to focus on his goal, which was fast approaching.

Hakon turned to Arinborg, who was standing by his side, her pretty dark eyebrows raised, her brown eyes angry.

"What did you say, Princess?"

"I said, I hope you have something in mind to soften the blow. He is convinced we are already married."

Hakon clenched his jaw. He had something in mind that would turn the blow into a storm.

"Do not worry, Princess. Your father will forgive me once he finds out that he will have the honor of marrying us."

She turned to the ship and muttered, "If you think it will make him forgive you, you clearly do not know him."

Hakon cocked his head. "Maybe so."

She gently cupped his jaw and turned his face towards her. She was lovely—dark arched eyebrows; big beautiful eyes; full lips, red and inviting. She was as tall as Mia, but bigger chested. Any man would give up freedom, lands, and silver to be the husband of a beautiful, strong, smart princess.

But her touch made Hakon want to step away, made him miss Mia's touch even more. This woman was not the woman his heart beat for.

The princess traced his cheekbone with her thumb. "I agreed to marry you even after what you did. But it does not mean I am ready to forgive you. That imposter is gone. That is a good beginning."

Hakon's fists clenched at Arinborg's foul words.

"But what would you do to make me forgive you?" she said in a husky voice, her eyes turning as dark as night, shining with special meaning. She knew what she was doing. She knew the effect she had on men and she assumed she'd have the same one on Hakon.

She would have.

If his heart, his body, and his soul did not belong to Mia.

Hakon had stood alone on the shore of the fjord after Mia

had left him, as weak as a sail robbed of wind. It had already been night when he'd gone back to the mead hall, thunderstruck, not seeing where he was going. And somehow, just as he was about to open the gates to the hall, his feet had carried him to his horse. He'd straddled him and flown after Mia. How could he have let her go alone into the woods? She might be in danger from wolves or the bear.

He was not ready to let her go, not ready to lose her. That could not have been the last time he ever saw her. The possibility hit him like a falling mountain.

But when he got to the sacred grove, she was nowhere to be seen. There were barely visible imprints in the soil and freshly pressed grass. He looked around for her, for any signs of an animal attack or of her hiding somewhere in case she changed her mind. But she was truly gone.

And now, in her place, was another. A beautiful woman who wanted him.

A beautiful woman he did not want.

A beautiful woman who was not Mia.

"Anything you would like me to," he finally answered. He had to make sure she gave King Nyr the impression that she was content.

Arinborg bit her full lip, a gesture that would have brought blood to his loins before. She shifted slightly towards him so that her breasts touched his arm, and he had to stop himself before he flinched.

Would he live like that the rest of his life? Pretending to like her when he could only think of Mia?

The thought made his whole body hurt.

He reminded himself that it was all for his goal, to get revenge on Nyr. And what happened after did not matter.

But if he was honest with himself, he did not believe that anymore.

The longship arrived and docked, and King Nyr descended. Rich furs framed his shoulders, gold and silver on his neck. His face was impassive, studying Hakon and Arinborg.

"Happy and healthy, Daughter, Son," Nyr said in way of greeting, and Hakon suppressed the urge to throw himself at the man and tear him apart.

"Happy and healthy, Father," said Arinborg, and Nyr nodded and looked at Hakon, expecting a welcome.

Hakon let a breath out. He had to win a bit more time. Then he would finish him. That was the agreement he had come to with his allies—Hakon would invite Nyr to visit his daughter, and then kill him while the other jarls were raiding his borg.

"Welcome." He gestured to the village and let Nyr pass first, joining him at the king's left shoulder.

"I trust all went well with your wedding?" Nyr said.

Arinborg, who walked to his right side, said, "We are not married yet, Father."

Nyr stopped at the border of the wooden pier and the rocky shore. "What?"

His eyes flickered between Hakon and Arinborg.

"Do not tell me you do not want him!" he thundered at Arinborg.

"I do." She blushed and looked down.

"Then why?"

"I fell and cut my ankle open on a slippery rock in a brook on the way to Lomdalen. I got a rot-wound and had to stay in a village until it healed. I was delirious and weak, so I could not send a messenger. I only arrived a week ago."

Nyr turned towards the village and walked on, and everyone followed. "I need a horn of mead. In Odin's name, you should have just wed as soon as you arrived. Why did you not?"

Arinborg pursed her lips and said nothing. So Hakon

answered. "Because I was married to someone who had identified herself as your daughter. And Arinborg was not sure if she wanted to marry me after that. But I convinced her."

Nyr spun, his fur cloak flying around him. *"What?"*

"It was an imposter, Father. She is gone."

"You married an imposter?" Nyr yelled. "How could you do that? Are you that stupid, Hakon? No, you are not. It is still your curse that attracts all sorts of bad luck, is it not, Beast?"

Hakon growled.

The insult hit him right where it hurt. Rage rose in him like a wave of fire, and his sword was in his hand.

That was it.

With a movement as light as a feather, the edge of the sword pointed right at Nyr's throat. Nyr's eyes widened in surprise, Arinborg gasped, and Nyr's and Hakon's men drew their weapons.

"What are you doing, fool?" Nyr spat.

Fury still roaring in Hakon, revenge tasted sweet at the tip of his sword. Finally, the moment had come.

"Something I have wanted to do ever since my father told me the truth. Kill the worm that poisoned everything."

As he said the word "poison," Mia's words came to mind. *You are drinking the poison of revenge, and you don't even realize that you are the one dying.*

Hakon's grip weakened. He could kill the man now. Just a slight pressure on his sword would do it.

But what next?

Most likely, Hakon would die fighting. His men would die, too, along with the women and children of his village. After all that Mia had done to keep them alive.

And he would not be able to help Mia and her baby.

He would truly drink the poison. It was not sweet. It was

bitter. And he did not want to do this anymore. His mother had died sacrificing her life out of love for him. He was not cursed.

He was blessed.

If he were to do this, kill King Nyr now, that sacrifice would be in vain, and he would turn that blessing into a curse with his own hands.

Because he was wrong about his purpose. He had thought revenge would bring back that happiness, that love he had felt when his mother was alive. But now he saw that revenge would not bring him any of that.

Mia did.

And now she was in terrible danger.

Maybe he was a beast, but Mia had healed him, repaired the wound to his soul. And now he needed to save the woman he loved from a true monster.

Hakon said, "But I won't do it."

He withdrew the sword, but still held it so that Nyr would not think to move against him. Hakon backed towards the woods.

"Do not think to attack the village, Nyr," he said.

"Ah, what shall stop me?"

"My allies are sieging your borg right now."

Nyr's face paled. "What?"

"It was a diversion, agreeing to marry Arinborg, while I made an alliance with three other jarls to kill you. They will stop your expansion, take your lands, and one of them will be the next king. You'd better hurry back home, save whatever you can."

He had not planned to tell Nyr that. But it was the only way to prevent him and his warriors from attacking the village. And Hakon knew Nyr would arrive too late to stop his allies even if he left now.

"So what will it be, Nyr? Fight us and lose your kingdom and your life, or go back and try to save both?"

Nyr snarled and gestured for his men to go back to the ship. He hurried there with long strides.

"Father! What about me?" Arinborg cried.

"You have done enough!" Nyr stopped and looked back at her. "You failed the only task that your life is worthy of."

Then he ran to the ship.

"You will not be harmed here," Hakon said. "Stay as long as you wish. But I will not marry you. I love someone else."

He found Torfi. "I am leaving to recover Mia, the healer who saved your wife and daughter from the coughing disease. I do not know if or when I will return. You are in charge in my stead. If I do not return, consider yourself the next jarl."

He squeezed the man's shoulder. Torfi nodded, solemn.

Hakon ran to the great hall where he took his ax and his shield, and then he ran towards the woods, towards the rock with runes, towards the woman he loved more than life itself.

CHAPTER TWENTY-ONE

Boston, September 5, 2019

Darkness surrounded Hakon. Or maybe he was the darkness. When he'd placed his hands on the rough surface, he had felt as if the rock was sucking him into Helheim, spinning him like a spindle, and then he had stopped existing.

He was born again, except he could not see. When was the "then" and when was the "now"? He did not know.

Finally, he emerged. First, he noticed the strange smell. Something acrid, as if whale oil had been burned for a long time. Nothing that smelled of trees or grass or earth. Then, he noticed the sound of water splashing against wood and rocks —something he would recognize anywhere. And there was a deep rumbling, as if a thousand small thunder storms were rolling back and forth. Screeching, voices, and music made his head pound.

Then his vision returned, and the light blinded him. It was

warm. Hot. The ground under his shoes radiated heat like an oven. The air carried the humidity of the sea.

He was sitting. His fingertips felt the surface of smooth, warm wood. When his eyes got used to the light, he jumped up, his hand on the handle of the ax.

Everywhere around him were stone houses. Perfectly square, dark red, as tall as mountains. There were square glass windows of such transparency that it seemed there was nothing there at all. He was standing on ground that consisted of smooth stones of equal size. It seemed, everything around him was stone.

In front of him was a square harbor, and in it, several docks and many, many ships. They were made of something that resembled white iron. Many of them had no masts and looked like giant birds' beaks.

Odin, Allfather, Mia had spoken true. She was from the future.

And now Hakon was in it.

The world after Ragnarok.

His breath rushing in and out, he looked around himself for danger, for any warriors that would see him as an intruder, any beasts that would want to attack. He kept his hand on the handle of the ax in warning. He did not take the weapon in his hand—he wanted to show that he came in peace. He came for his woman.

People were passing by, sitting on benches with backs that were facing the water. Hakon had never been in such heat as this, and he did not question why women wore such short trousers and skirts, their legs bare. Their tunics were tight around their bosoms and waists. Men wore short pants to the knee, or above, light tunics with sleeves that ended at their shoulders, and shoes that seemed to only have soles and thin straps that went between or over the toes.

No one seemed to be disturbed by him, so he straightened, let his hand loosen, and looked around trying to understand how he could find Mia.

People stared at him as they were passing by. One man who had his arm around a woman's shoulders said with a chuckle, "Cool costume, bro."

Hakon stared back and scowled. He had no idea what the meaning of the phrase was. He only understood that something about him seemed cold to the man, and based on his chuckle, he approved of it. Hakon was not surprised, he would approve of anything cold in this heat, too.

People who sat on the benches looked at black squares in their hands, and some passersby pointed them at Hakon. Sensing danger, he took his ax out, ready for an attack, but no one launched at him. On the contrary, people were relaxed, discussing something while looking at him. Some of them were smiling. They held the strange objects not as weapons, with sharp edges pointed at him, but rather as shields, flat side towards him. They looked greatly entertained.

He must look strange to them, with his wolf cloak, his baggy pants, and his long linen tunic.

Or maybe their amusement had something to do with his coolness.

No matter. He had not come for them. He had come for Mia.

If Dan had her, he needed to find him first. But where? His mouth went as dry as the hot rocks he was standing on. Worry flipped in his gut like a deep-water fish.

Then he remembered something Mia said—Dan had named a boat after her. He even ran his affairs from there. Perhaps like a king in his stronghold, Hakon thought.

Hakon had to find a boat called *Mia*.

He looked around the harbor. How would he know what the boat was called?

But then he saw strange runes on the ships. And he understood what they said. *Joy. Adrianna. Sunset. Emily. Boston.*

Boston! Mia had mentioned this was where she lived. This was the right place.

He turned around and saw an old man with a bald head, circles of glass on his nose, studying him carefully.

"Good man!" Hakon said, and slammed his mouth shut. He was speaking a foreign language. The feeling of his jaw muscles and tongue moving in a different way was like putting on someone else's armor. It did not quite fit. Was it like this for Mia when she spoke his tongue?

He returned his attention to the man in front of him. "Where can I find a boat called *Mia*?"

The man took a small step back, his eyes wide, and held his hands up. "I have no money on me. I can't give you money for your performance."

Hakon scowled. "I do not need your money. Tell me where to find *Mia*."

He glanced to Hakon's left and pointed at something. "Isn't that *Mia*?"

Hakon's gut jumped, and he followed the direction the man was pointing, hoping maybe by some miracle Mia herself would be standing there. But she wasn't. Behind the tallest and thickest longhouse he had ever seen, made out of the same dark-red bricks as the rest of them, there was another harbor like this one. There, he saw the smooth white stern of a giant boat. And on the side were three runes: *M I A*.

The Norn's magic in the stone had sent him to the right place. The fury that had always been his friend on the battlefield began simmering in his blood.

He left the man and walked along the stone quay. The

roaring grew louder, and between the giant houses he saw something that made him stop dead. Iron carriages with roofs were driving on their own at a speed that even a horse could not manage. What was this strange magic?

Hakon clenched his jaw. He was a warrior. He had looked death in the eye countless times, and yet all these things he could not explain put bone-deep fear in him.

That was what it must have been like for Mia, to arrive in his world, no explanation, no reason for it, not knowing where she was, if the next person she saw was friend or foe. And she was with child. So he must have terrified her when he had swept in and thrown her onto his horse and then told her she was there to marry him.

And then she had thought to stay.

She must really love him.

Hakon sped up. The boat *Mia* was the only thing he saw, no number of miraculous carts, houses with windows, or boats without masts and sails could distract him from getting her back. Especially if she needed help.

He went through an iron gate with runes spelling "Marina" on top, down an iron ramp and onto the wooden docks where many other boats were docked. He sped towards the boat at the very end.

There was a small ramp leading onboard, and as soon as he stepped on it, a man in a thin black jacket and black trousers appeared from the doorway. Unarmed, as far as Hakon could see.

"Who are you?" the man demanded.

He must be a guard. Hakon knew that if they had boats of iron and fast-moving carts, most likely their weapons would be as surprising and as efficient. He had to be careful.

"I am cool, bro," he said, and the words were like magic. A surprised smile touched the man's face and he looked Hakon up and down, relaxing a little. People from the future did appreciate the cold.

"Yeah?" the man said. "Is boss waitin' for ye or somethin'? Did Mia hire an entertainer? She's been readin' a lot about Vikings ever since we found her."

Hakon clenched his fists and a low growl escaped his throat. His face must have changed because the guard frowned, careful.

"Gettin' in the role, I see. Hold on, I'll ask the boss."

"No need, bro. They will want to be surprised," Hakon said.

"Nah. Hold on. Hey, Mia!" he yelled. "Mia!"

"What is it, Carl?" Hakon heard a muffled male voice from inside.

"Boss? Did she hire a Viking actor?"

"Very funny!" Mia's voice this time, and Hakon's heart began thumping like it had not since she left him.

"He's here—if you did."

"What?"

"He's here, the Viking! Lookin' real. Should I let him in?"

Hakon heard steps, metallic bangs. Then her face appeared out of the entrance to what looked like a small house on the boat. His breath caught in his gut, the world faded, and all he could see was her. That was it. He knew now why the Norn had sent her to him through more than a thousand years.

Because she was a healer, and the parts of his heart, of his soul, that were broken, lonely, and rejected began healing into one whole.

If he died today defending her, or if she rejected him, it was all worth it just to see her for one moment.

Mia's eyes widened in shock as they met his, then he saw tenderness, then fear. She glanced down into the ship. "I'll be right back, Dan!" she said, then emerged.

She was in a floating, dancing, light dress—something

similar to what she had been wearing when he had found her by the rune rock. Her belly had grown slightly, and she looked beautiful and gentle. Hakon wanted to take her in his arms and bury his face in her hair.

She walked towards him. "It's all right, Carl," she said.

"Who is it, Mia?" a male voice rang from somewhere inside the boat, then Hakon heard footsteps.

"Come behind me, Mia," Hakon said, stretching his arm out, even though she was still on the boat and had not even passed Carl.

Carl, probably sensing something was wrong, put one hand into the opening of his jacket, and Hakon dropped his hand onto the handle of his ax.

A man appeared from behind Mia, and everything stood still. He was wearing a similar jacket and pants to Carl, but gray. He was tall, dark haired, and behind the mask of polite hospitality, danger glared at Hakon.

He had seen that look in the eyes of rare men. He had seen it in Nyr's eyes.

The eyes of a man who would stop at nothing to get what he wanted.

They fell on Hakon, and a muscle on Hakon's cheek jerked. He gripped the ax.

Dan met his gaze, his fingers clasped around Mia's upper arm, and he pulled her against him. Hakon's gut twisted.

"And who is this, Mia?" Dan asked.

"I am Hakon the Beast," Hakon said. "And I have come to take back my wife."

CHAPTER TWENTY-TWO

All of Mia's breath was sucked out of her lungs.

He'd come for her, through time. He wanted to take her home. He forgave her.

Every cell of her body became alive, crackling with sparks of joy. Seeing Hakon again was a miracle. Seeing him here, in Boston, in 2019, was even more bewildering than when she'd traveled through time herself.

"You got married?" Dan turned to Mia, killing her delight, his face blank. "To *him*?"

Between her and the man she loved, was the man who'd captured her. Mia nodded, and Dan's face became a cold stone mask. Ice water flooded Mia's veins. Dan's men had found her right after she had appeared at her apartment and had taken her to Dan. But funny enough, Dan was afraid of her after she'd disappeared into thin air right in front of him. He had asked her once if she was a witch, and she hadn't given him any explanation, which had made him even more cautious. He hadn't touched her, hadn't said a single rude word to her since. This was the first time he had touched her since she got back.

"Please come inside, *Hakon*," Dan said and gestured for Hakon to do so.

Mia's neck stiffened. No!

"No. I came for my wife, and she is leaving with me."

Dan pulled Mia closer to himself, making her flinch. The cold barrel of a gun pressed against her ribs, and all the blood drained from her face. Hakon's eyebrows snapped together, his eyes narrowing and darkening, turning into amber, like a wolf on the hunt.

"Let's not air our dirty laundry out here," Dan said. "Come inside."

Hakon nodded in cold agreement and walked across the ramp and onboard the ship. Mia's knees turned to jelly as she watched him walking into enemy territory, alone, right into a trap. What could his ax and sword do against a gun?

Carl straightened but only followed Hakon with his eyes. Mia knew the price of that attention all too well. Carl looked like a goofball, but he wouldn't hesitate if he needed to protect his boss at the cost of another man's life. Mia's feet turned to ice despite the warm day.

Dan gestured for Hakon to go into the cabin and then one floor down to where the bedrooms and his study were. When they entered Dan's study, the smell of wood and polish enveloped them. A massive mahogany desk stood by the far wall, along with a giant leather chair. To the right were a conference table and eight chairs. By the left wall, a leather couch. A Persian rug added to the impression of tasteful opulence.

Dan closed the door behind him, still gripping Mia's arm, and pointed the gun at Hakon. Mia's hands shook as Hakon studied the gun with an amused expression, probably thinking such a small thing couldn't be dangerous enough to do any real damage.

Hakon must have sensed some danger, though, as his hand tightened on the handle of his ax.

"No, my friend," Dan said. Mia's throat clenched. She knew that tone. Dan talked like that to his employees when they had done something wrong. Employees Mia would never see again. "I doubt they're real, but hands off your Viking toys."

He walked to the table, dragging Mia after him, then sat on the edge, stretching out his legs and crossing his ankles.

Hakon looked into Mia's eyes, and she saw love shining back at her, and she finally began getting warmer. "Are you all right?" he said.

"Yes." She managed a smile that she meant to be reassuring. "You shouldn't have come."

"And the babe?"

Dan's face turned livid. "The *babe* is my concern. It's my child."

Hakon's face lost all tenderness as he looked at Dan, steel in his eyes. "Maybe so. But it is mine just the same."

Dan's clean-shaven jaw tightened. "Who are you, anyway, *Hakon the Beast*? Are you a wrestler? A stripper? Jason Momoa's stunt double or something?"

Hakon looked at Mia. "How much does he know?"

"Nothing," she said.

He nodded, turning his attention to Dan, who looked both confused and furious at the exchange. "I am someone you should be terrified of," Hakon said. He looked at Dan from under his eyebrows with cold fire in his eyes, and a chill ran through Mia. For the first time, she saw why Hakon was known as the Beast. She would not want to be the one he looked at like that.

"*Terrified* of you?" Dan stood up, letting go of Mia, and she backed away from him. "You do not come to my boat and threaten *me*. Do you know who I am?"

"I do. You are a bristle on Loki's sweaty ass. You are the runs that a forest troll has after eating a rotten corpse. You are the offal that makes even pigs want to vomit."

Dan's face was reddening, and Mia's hands shook. The angrier Dan got, the more unpredictable he'd become.

"No man should lay his hand on a woman," Hakon said. "No man should make her suffer. And yet, you did. So you are no man."

Dan was shaking now, his eyes narrowed, the corners of his mouth crawled down. Mia's fingernails bit into the flesh of her palms. *We'll get through this, peanut. I will not let any harm come to you or Daddy.*

And she did not mean Dan.

"You fucker," Dan growled, pointing the gun at Hakon.

Mia took a step towards him, her hands trembling. "No! Dan, don't!"

"Mia, stand back." Hakon's hand was still on the handle of his ax. "Do you want me to kill him?"

"What? No! Of course not."

Hakon nodded. "As you wish." He looked at Dan. "You deserve to die a thousand deaths for every time you caused her any pain. But I will not kill you if she does not wish it. So. Let us resolve this peacefully. Mia is coming with me today. What will it take for you to let her go?"

Dan's upper lip crawled up, turning his face into a predator's snarl. Mia couldn't breathe. This would not end peacefully. Hakon was just making Dan angrier and angrier, and he did not know what the man was capable of.

"You're delirious if you think I will let the mother of my child go," Dan said.

"What do you want? I doubt it is treasure—it looks like you have plenty."

Dan's mouth turned into a straight line. "I. Want. My. Child. And my woman. Now, either fuck off or I *will* kill you."

Hakon arched his brow and looked pointedly at the gun. "With that?"

Oh no! He'll get himself killed! The cold worry that had snaked around her stomach exploded, shooting ice water into her veins. "Hakon, it's a gun!" Mia cried. "It shoots bullets. It's deadly. Leave. Go back before he does something."

Hakon frowned and studied the weapon, then slowly removed his ax from his belt.

"Put it away," Dan said, "or I will shoot you."

"Try," Hakon said, and darted down for Dan's legs.

The gun fired with a deafening pop. Mia screamed. Terror gripped her body like a steel fist. Hakon hugged Dan's legs and pushed him. Dan fell, and another blast filled the room with an acrid, chemical smell. Hakon pressed Dan's gun arm to the floor. With the other hand, he pressed the blade of his ax against Dan's throat.

"If you do not wish to let her go peacefully, you will let her go because I made you. Mia, leave."

"Not so fast." Dan's gun arm twitched.

The barrel was pointed at Mia. The floor shifted under her feet, and she covered her belly protectively.

"You will not," Hakon snarled.

Oh, he would. He was capable of anything to save himself.

"One twitch and I will," Dan's voice rasped.

A low growl escaped Hakon's throat.

"Stand up slowly," Dan said.

Hakon obeyed, got to his feet and backed away. Mia's mouth filled with a sour taste.

Dan stood up. "Now put your ax and your sword on the floor and kick them towards me."

Hakon did as asked. His weapons flew across the carpet at

Dan's feet and landed just two steps from Mia. She had a hard time swallowing the jagged rock in her throat.

Dan pointed the gun at Hakon, and everything froze.

Mia knew then that this would be it. Dan would kill Hakon. It was bad enough he had taken away her freedom to work as a doctor and her baby's chance to grow up as a normal member of society and not part of the criminal world.

But now he was about to take away the man she loved.

Her whole life, she had been at the whim of men—first her father, then Dan. Hakon, too, in the beginning.

Enough! Anger roared deep in Mia's gut like a wall of fire. She would not let the man who had ruined her life take away her last glimpse of happiness.

She sank to her knees and took Hakon's sword. It was heavy. Too heavy. But anger gave her more strength than she knew she had. Maybe it was the years of battle fury that the sword had drunk in, but it vibrated in her hands ever so slightly. And maybe it was the fury born inside of her, but her arms filled with strength, adrenaline running through her veins like electricity through cables.

Her body took over. It knew what to do, as if something ancient in her blood urged her to protect the ones she loved. Every cell of her body screamed, *no more!* No more tyranny, no more abuse, no more allowing some man to take away the things she loved. Her legs assumed a strong position, her arms pointing the sword at Dan's back.

Mia had just opened her mouth to order Dan to drop the gun, when Hakon lunged forward like a giant flash of fur and man. Dan staggered and leaped back. The gun exploded in his hand in a bright flash of fire and smoke. Mia squeezed her eyes closed just as she was propelled back from the sudden impact. But she stayed on her feet.

When she opened her eyes she saw blood. Dan's blood,

welling around the sword, the edge of which had sunk into his back, right where his heart was.

Dan yelped and turned, eyes wild and bewildered as he looked at her. His mouth moved soundlessly, his arms waving, trying to grab her. But his heart was already failing. His eyes rolled, and he fell forward onto his stomach, lifeless.

Mia's breath came out ragged, her body numb. She should feel remorse. She should feel guilty. She had just killed a man.

But instead she had more space in her chest to breathe. A weight had been lifted off her shoulders, and the vise that had always gripped her stomach in fear had disappeared. She remembered every time he'd hit her, every time she'd flown against the wall from his hands—and that one time when he had taken her against her will, the most painful time of all.

No more.

She was free.

Did Vikings feel that way when they killed their enemies?

Hakon was studying her with such tenderness that her heart squeezed. He was also holding his shoulder.

"Oh gosh, are you all right?" She hurried to him and removed his hand from his shoulder, but he brought her into a bear hug, his warmth, his smell enveloping her.

"A scratch. I am proud of you, my Valkyrie," he whispered in her hair, then looked into her face. "You are a Viking."

Mia smiled at that, then glanced back at Dan's body. "We need to get out of here."

"Yes. Let us go home."

CHAPTER TWENTY-THREE

"How do we find the Norn?" Hakon said against Mia's hair.

Her scent in his nostrils was honey, and he was drunk with it, swimming in it. She was in his arms, her round belly pressing gently into his stomach. Her body was warm.

"God, I missed you," she whispered, then inhaled against his tunic.

"I could not breathe without you."

She raised her head to look him in the eyes. "Thank you for coming for me."

"I would come for you in the depths of Helheim."

She smiled. "I think you just did."

"I died a thousand deaths when you picked up the sword. A healer, a mother, and now a shield-maiden..."

His heart was so full of love for her, it was bigger than Midgard.

"Yours," she said, and their lips met, plunging him into a world of bliss, magic, and sweetness.

He wanted the moment to last for a whole lifetime, but it

could not. Mia withdrew, gently, her chest rising and falling quickly against his ribcage.

"I'd love to pick this up soon, but for now, we need to go," Mia said. She looked back at Dan's body and slipped out of Hakon's arms. A small sting of disappointment pierced him. "I don't know where we can find the Norn, but I know we can't stay here for much longer. Dan's study is soundproof, but Carl might come check soon. He was alone this morning, but that's unusual. More guards will probably arrive soon. We need to be far away by the time they find Dan."

Hakon nodded, then walked to Dan's body and removed his sword. He wiped the blood off on Dan's jacket and picked up his ax. Mia opened the door and peered out. Then looked back at him, her eyebrows high.

"We don't need to look for the Norn. She's already here."

Hakon frowned, and the blood in his veins stood still.

He was about to meet one of the Norns, who knew the fates of every person, every god, and every creature in all nine worlds of Yggdrasil. Odin himself was in their power. They had even predicted Ragnarok, the end of the world.

He had never heard of anyone who had met a Norn, besides Mia. Not even in legends.

And now he would meet one of these powerful, mystical beings. Their fate was in her hands. Would she send them back? Would she say that his destiny lay here, in the future? Would she take his life?

Whatever his destiny was—whatever *their* destiny was— he would meet it the same way he had always gone into battle and the same way he lived his life.

With his head high.

Hakon straightened and followed Mia through the door.

At the bottom of the stairs sat a small old woman dressed in the clothes of the future. She was knitting, with a serene smile. As if there was no dead body in the next room. As if there was no guard upstairs. And as if there was no danger that more guards would come for them.

Hakon stopped next to Mia who was standing by the stairs and staring at the woman. Without looking at him, she took his hand and squeezed. His heart began beating more calmly.

"Ah." The Norn glanced at them with curiosity. "The supposedly married couple. I like your tapestry. You did well."

"Can you send us back home?" Hakon asked.

She stopped knitting, stood up, and walked to him. Her timeless blue eyes met his, and a shiver ran through him. The feeling was familiar. He knew it from the battlefield, when destiny saturated the very air—it was in the scent of blood, in the flash of iron, in the sound of pierced flesh and broken bone. When every movement, every breath, and every step determined if you lived or died.

That was what he saw in her eyes. Countless deaths and births. Wars, the rise and fall of kings, the discoveries of new lands, new worlds, and new creatures. He saw happiness and despair. Love and indifference. Bravery and cowardice.

He saw his destiny.

"I can send you back home," the Norn said.

A hummingbird began fluttering its wings right where Mia's heart was. Home...

Ever since she'd traveled back in time, her life had been filled with miracles. Today was the capstone. Hakon had come for her through time. He loved her, he forgave her, and he wanted her.

And she had finally stood up to Dan.

She was free.

Her shoulders straightened, the tension in them evaporating. Every cell of her body was full of energy. *I am enough*, the voice in her head sang.

Mia remembered her mother—her obedience, her docility—and she wished that she could give her mother the gift of strength and independence that now radiated within her like a warm, glowing ball of light. That it would fill the gaps in her mother's soul, fill her cells with the energy and love that she was lacking.

Because Mia was enough.

Enough for her. Enough for her baby. She would not allow anyone to dictate to her, or to her son, how she should live her life.

She was going to define it on her own.

And then she knew that her own life was not back in the Viking Age.

If she was going to define her and her baby's life, it would not be without modern medical care, safety, and security.

Pain exploded in her chest, in her gut, in every part of her. Because that meant her life would be without Hakon.

The Norn turned to Mia, and in the sweet old lady she had met for the first time in the hospital cafeteria, she now saw someone else. Something else. Something that chilled her body.

Destiny.

But not hers.

"Do you want to go?" the Norn said.

She rummaged in her purse and removed the golden spindle.

Hakon inhaled sharply. "Never did I think I would see the golden spindle with my own eyes," he said, his voice low and solemn.

Mia turned to him. The words that she was about to say

tasted bitter on her tongue. "I am not coming with you, Hakon."

His face... The change in it echoed inside of her as though the sword she had killed Dan with cut her own heart in two. The happiness, the joy, the wonder were gone, replaced by loss and despair.

"What?" he croaked.

Mia squeezed his hands. "I am sorry. I must stay in my own time. I can't have a life back in the Viking Age."

"But you said you wanted to be with me—"

Mia could not breath. A fist clasped her lungs and twisted. "I was wrong. Now that I am free of Dan, for the first time in my life, I feel like I am the real me. The me that I was always supposed to be. I can finally live my life. I can give my baby the best future he can have. Just the two of us. I want to finish the residency program. I want to become a doctor. I want to raise him in love, in safety, and in prosperity."

"I can give you all of that. I will protect you. Not that you need much protection. I will give you more riches than you can imagine. And you know no one will love you and our son more than I."

Mia's soul was being torn apart. "I know." She took her hands from his. He tried to hold them longer but then let go. Mia took one step back, and an abyss spread between them.

"But love is not everything. I have just gained independence. I need to figure out my life...our life"—she put her hand on her bump and felt a reassuring kick—"on my own."

Hakon inhaled raggedly, as if he could not get enough oxygen. Without glancing at the Norn, he stretched out his hand. "Send me back. Now. Before I begin to beg her or take her with me by force."

Mia glanced at the Norn. Her face wore the same amused,

curious expression, a half smile on her lips, as if Mia's and Hakon's lives had not just ended.

"Interesting choice, Mia," the Norn said. "As you wish, Hakon."

She put the spindle in his hand.

Mia reached out, as though to stop him, as the image of him began evaporating like steam. Her whole body hurt as though a thousand hammers were hitting her. Their eyes were locked, and even though she had just ended their happiness, his eyes were full of tenderness, connected with hers.

"I love you," he said soundlessly.

And then he was gone.

CHAPTER TWENTY-FOUR

Denver, October 18, 2019

Mia wobbled slightly on the sunlit driveway to the front door of her house, bags of groceries in her arms. It was a cold October afternoon, and her breath rushed out in quick streams of steam.

The Rocky Mountains were gorgeous on the far side of the horizon, tall and white and dreamy. The sight of them made her heart stop every time she looked at them, reminding her of other mountains, the ones where she had been truly happy for the first time in her life.

Mia turned away and unlocked the door.

She had lived in the house for about six weeks now, and the smell of old furniture still hung in the air. She had rented it furnished, and it was obvious that before her no one had been living there for years. It was also obvious that the previous tenants had been old.

She set the groceries on the kitchen counter and paused for

a second, leaning with her hands against the countertop, her chin on her chest. She studied her bump, which had grown round and cute at the end of her second trimester. She remembered Hakon caressing it and referring to the baby as his. As always when something reminded her of Hakon, the pain and heartache rushed over her like a tsunami, choking her, deafening her, blinding her with a blackness that was ready to swallow everything.

She forced herself to breathe in and out, counting to four. Little by little, the darkness let her go, and she could look around, taking in the normality. The old, chipped brown kitchen, the fridge that always smelled no matter how well she cleaned it, the yellow lace curtains on the window.

Was this better than the warmth of the hearth in Hakon's mead hall? The smell of freshly cooked stew? The humming of the women as they spun wool and weaved sails? Hakon's strong arms around her, his heartbeat against her palm, his rich, low voice saying that he loved her?

Mia shook her head, tears burning her eyes.

No. No need to regret anything. She had chosen this. She had known she would need to lie low, take on a new life under a fake name—ironically for the second time in her life, but this time forever. She had known she would need to give up love. She had known she would never be a happy woman in this life. No man could make her happy except Hakon.

When Hakon had disappeared back to his time, the Norn had said Carl would not notice her, so she needed to go now if she wanted to escape. Mia hadn't waited another moment. She had rushed to her old apartment where she had the money and the fake ID she had prepared when she'd wanted to escape Dan in June.

She hadn't taken a flight, afraid she would leave too many traces. She'd bought a used car in the suburbs of Boston and just taken off, her mind blank, her nerves numb, her fingers shaking.

She had just begun a residency program at the University of Colorado, and the job was a welcome, blissful tornado of activity that sucked all her thoughts, energy, and attention away from the raw, pulsing, throbbing wound in her chest.

Mia let out a long breath, wiped her tears away and straightened up. She was hungry, as always since her second trimester had started. She needed to cook something to keep her baby healthy.

Fish tacos today. She'd eat them alone, just like every dinner for the past two months, with the TV on to keep her company. The joys of modern life.

You chose it, she reminded herself as she stabbed the plastic wrapping of the frozen cod. *You wanted to take control of your life. So there you go. This is your life. Enjoy.*

You could have gone with him, another part of her said. *He wanted you. He came for you through time, risking everything.*

Everything.

And she had rejected him. She had stayed, and he had not tried to control her. He had respected her decision even if it hurt him deeply.

Mia removed the fish from the wrapping, the frozen fillets burning her fingers, and put it on the plate to defrost in the microwave.

Hakon loved her too much to put her in another cage.

Not that she would have let him.

He would rather be unhappy for his whole life than force her to be with him. And she wanted to be with him so much...

But it was impossible. She had made her choice. She was doing it for her baby.

It had been confirmed at her last ultrasound—she was having a boy. She imagined the life they would have. Mia, tired, forcing a smile, focusing on her son as if he were the only joy in her life. She would be half human, half ragged wound. She wanted the best life for him.

But would seeing his mother like that be the best for him? Growing up and learning that life was about sacrifice. That safety was the most important thing.

Was it, though?

Mia had thought she was taking control of her life. But it wasn't control, was it?

It was misery.

Mia held her breath as an idea struck her.

Why did she assume that it was either one or the other?

Hope lit her fingers and toes up like little firecrackers and sent sparks up her arms and legs.

No, don't hope yet. Maybe it won't work.

But if it didn't work, she'd find another way.

She picked up her car keys and a bag of peeled baby carrots and headed for the door, abandoning the fish in the microwave.

Her breath catching in her throat, she whispered, "I'm coming, Hakon."

Of course the Norn wasn't in the cafeteria of UCHealth.

Desperation crept through Mia as she realized the Norn would not make it too easy for her. She had rejected one chance to go back in time. There may not be another.

One heart-wrenching week passed, and Mia was nowhere near finding the Norn.

Then, one evening, Mia opened the door to her car and almost fell to the ground when she saw someone in the passenger seat. Mia jumped, clasping her hands to her chest.

"Oh my god!" she yelled as she settled in the driver's seat, glaring at the Norn. "I'm pregnant for pity's sake. Couldn't you have just waited next to the car?"

The Norn laughed. It was a bit strange to see a being who determined the destinies of gods and men laugh. Mia didn't know if that happened often, but the laugh was sweet, a little bit girlish, pure, and full of joy. The old lady almost snorted.

"Ah, humans." The Norn wiped one eye and pressed out a couple of last giggles. "You are adorable. Anyways, you were looking for me. I thought I'd save you some time, given your"—she looked pointedly at Mia's bump—"situation. What do you have in mind?"

Mia exhaled. She had prepared for a negotiation, but now she had been taken completely off guard, and she needed a moment to remember what she wanted to say. But her thoughts scattered like beads off a broken necklace string.

"Ehm," Mia said. "I want to go back to Hakon."

"Do you now? Came to your senses, didn't you?"

"I did. Can you send me back?"

"Your tapestry certainly shines when you are together. You bring out the best in each other. I enjoy your story."

Mia smiled, and one huge part of the rock on her chest lifted off. But not all.

"Well," Mia said. "The thing is, it's not about just me anymore, is it?" She gently put her hand on her bump. "If I go back, I don't leave a choice for my baby. I'm making the decision for him. And I don't think it's fair."

"Parents move cities, countries all the time."

"It's not exactly like that. Cities and countries still have more or less the same medical development, well, compared to medieval times anyways. Vaccinations, antibiotics, and hospitals are pretty much available. I am taking him not just through space but through time."

The Norn's eyes burned with curiosity, and she leaned forward. "So, you have a proposal for me, do you not?"

Mia swallowed hard. What would she do if the Norn said no to her request?

"Yes, I do have a proposal. I want to be able to go back and forth through time. Grant me a multiple-entry visa, if you please."

The Norn's eyes widened in surprise and indignation. "What?" she demanded.

Mia put her hands in front of herself protectively. "Only in case of emergencies! If my son gets sick with the plague or something."

The Norn crossed her arms over her chest. "You and him?"

"Yes. Only life and death situations, so that I can save his life."

"All right. Only once."

"Five times."

"Three."

"And one time for Hakon."

The Norn frowned. "Not for you?"

"No. I'll be fine. I need to protect my men."

"All right. Four times."

Mia nodded, then let out a long breath. The Norn studied her with a hint of amusement on her lips. "That is not all, is it?"

"No." Mia clasped her hands on the wheel and stared at them, then met the Norn's ancient eyes. "I don't want to rob my son of his choice. He was conceived here, but I am taking him back in time without asking him if he wants his future to be there. So, when he's eighteen, I want him to be able to decide if he wants to stay with us back in the Viking Age or go to the twenty-first century and live here."

The Norn raised her eyebrows. "I determine destinies. Don't you think I already know what he will decide?"

Mia raised her chin. "Did you know that I would not go with Hakon? And that I would then change my mind?"

The Norn smiled and only lifted her shoulder.

When she didn't say anything, Mia said, "No. I don't think that you know. I don't want to believe that everything is determined the day someone is born, like Norsemen believe. I think I am the one controlling my destiny."

The Norn shrugged. "Well, that is not completely true, is it? If it was so, you would never have traveled back in time and you would never have met Hakon. You would have still been in Dan's hands."

Mia frowned. "I suppose you're right. But I was the one who decided to grab the spindle."

"So, what will I have in return for allowing your son to have a choice and for you to travel in time four times?"

Mia gestured with her hands. "What would you like?"

"Hmmm." The Norn tapped on her lips with her index finger. "I would like you to sacrifice a goat at the rune stone in my honor every evening and to dance naked in the sacred grove every morning."

Mia's jaw dropped. "What?"

The Norn guffawed, clasping her thigh with one hand, snorting. "Just kidding, as you say these days. Look at your face!"

Mia exhaled and pretended to wipe sweat from her forehead. "Phew. You are on fire with jokes today, aren't you?"

The Norn let out a long, satisfied "Ahhh," then met Mia's eyes. "Sweetheart. The destinies of men and gods are often tragic. Hopeless. They never learn. I'm like a teacher. I have my favorites in the class. And you are one of them. You deserve happiness. So does Hakon. So does your child. I will agree to your terms if you agree to one of mine."

Mia's eyes blurred from tears. "Of course. What is it?"

The Norn leaned forward and squeezed Mia's hand. "Do not waste one moment of your life. Make every single one count. Do not let the gifts that I am giving you now go to waste. If you ever come to a similar choice, be sure you know what is right. Because I will not give you another chance."

Mia nodded enthusiastically, tears falling down her cheeks. "Don't you worry. I won't. I'm ready and packed. Please, send me back to my man."

CHAPTER TWENTY-FIVE

Lomdalen, Norway, October 25, 875 AD

Hakon stretched his hand out to the fire in the hearth, and its warmth touched his palm. The mead hall was silent, as if the very house held its breath. Half of the village must have gathered around the hearth tonight. Children, men, women, thralls, and servants. Solveig listened to him with a solemn face.

"What happened then, Jarl?" said Ledis, pulling at his fur cloak from where she sat on his lap.

Hakon blinked at her. Eight-year-old Ledis had been so afraid of him previously that she had dropped a basket of parsnips at the sight of him. It had been the day of the solstice. The day he had met Mia. The memory of Mia, the way he missed her, gripped his lungs, making it hard to breathe. This had been happening ever since he had come back. How was she? How was the babe? Hakon hoped she was happy and safe and that she was the healer she had wanted to be.

He exhaled a breath through his clenched throat, hoping he could breathe out the pain. Futile, of course.

Mia was always with him. She was part of him—his body, his soul, his everything.

"And then the Norn pulled out the golden spindle," Hakon said.

His people gasped, leaning closer. It was probably the tenth time he was telling them the story, and they still gasped every time he told it. One corner of Hakon's mouth curled up. Ever since he had come back, everything had changed. It was as if he had found himself in a new village. The scared glances, the silence towards him, the suppressed anger and fear of him, were gone.

That had started to change after Mia had given him that remedy against the curse. But everything had changed completely when he returned from the future. People appreciated and respected how he had dealt with King Nyr.

But they loved that he had gone through time into the future for Mia. They all loved Mia, even though she had assumed a different name. But she had saved many lives, and people did not forget that.

Finally, when Hakon had told them the whole truth—about Mia being a time traveler, the Norn who had sent her, and that Hakon himself had seen the Norn and talked to her—people had realized he could not have been cursed.

He was blessed. He was favored by the Norn herself.

He had seen the golden spindle.

He had touched it.

He had traveled through time and brought them knowledge of the future.

Ever since then, he had repeated the story of his journey at least twice a week, and every time more and more people came to listen.

"And how did it look?" Ledis asked.

"It was of pure gold, and there were carvings of the gods. I saw Fenrir, the giant wolf, and Yggdrasil, the world tree, and Odin and Freya. It was the most beautiful thing I have ever seen."

Except Mia.

People murmured, looked around, nodded, their eyes wide.

"And then?" Ledis said.

"And then—" his voice broke. "Mia said she wanted to stay in her time."

"I was a fool," Mia's voice said, and Hakon's heart burst from pain as if a thousand spears pierced it. He must be missing her so much he was starting to imagine things.

But he looked up in the direction of the voice, wondering who had spoken. And he stopped living for a moment. Because in the darkness of the hall, by the entrance gates, was a woman with a round belly. Hakon felt as if Thor himself had just struck him with Mjölnir. He could not see her face in the darkness, just the shape of her. Was she a spirit?

What seemed like an eternity later, when Hakon could think again, he put Ledis gently on her mother's lap and stood up, squinting, trying to see.

"Come closer, woman!" someone said. "He can't see you."

She moved forward, the orange light of the fire coloring her simple white apron dress. Hakon took in every movement—the gait, the way the skirts moved around her legs—were so painfully familiar. He could not allow himself to hope. She was wobbling a little bit now, her belly heavier and rounder.

And then when she was close enough for the fire to illuminate her face, he could no longer deny the truth.

"Mia," he rasped. It was all he could manage.

She smiled. "I was an idiot. I belong where you are."

Hakon could not move. His feet were like rocks. People

were looking at him. Then he felt someone tugging at the side of his trousers, and he looked down.

"Go," Ledis said. "She came back, do you not see?"

Hakon nodded. "I see."

He walked to Mia. People gave way to him when he stepped over the bench, and then as he walked past those who were standing behind it. Everyone was watching.

When he was standing right in front of her, his heart was banging against his ribcage like a ram.

"What does this mean, Mia?" he said. "Why are you here? Don't tell me you came just for one day. I won't survive if you leave me again."

She had never been as beautiful as she was now. She glowed from within, her radiance brighter than the light of the fire. He was hers. Enthralled by her. Belonging to her. At her mercy.

"I'm not leaving," she said, and it came out in a whisper. "If you'll have me—us. We'll stay where we belong."

Hakon's pulse thundered in his ears. "How can I trust you?" he said. "I came for you, you said you wanted me. And then you did not. I felt that I was dying then."

He saw the pain in her eyes, probably the same pain that he had felt every day without her. She was nodding, short, nervous nods. Then she went into the purse she had dropped on the floor when she entered. She brought out a small black box. Then she dropped to one knee, awkwardly because of her belly, and held the box out to him.

"What is this?" He stared at her and the box. "What are you doing?"

She opened the box, and on a black little pillow was a ring, black with a band of small rubies in the middle. As the firelight gleamed against it, he saw that in the middle, where the ruby band had a gap, the black metal became a wolf's snarling jaws.

Hakon looked at the ring, which was the most beautiful piece of jewelry he had ever seen.

"This is how people in my time propose," she said. "Hakon Ulfsson, will you marry me? Me, Mia, not Princess Arinborg. Or anyone else. Me."

He looked into her eyes, and in them, he saw everything. They shone with love and peace. And the peace and love he had been craving since his mother's death enveloped him, filling in the cracks in his heart.

He took her elbows and helped her to stand up, and she sighed in gratitude. She must be quite uncomfortable in her condition. "I will not allow my wife to be any lower than me," he said, and Mia beamed.

Her closeness sent a wave of warmth, like sunshine, through his blood. He drew her to him, the box with the ring still in her hand, and took her in his arms before she could evaporate like the last snow of winter. His lips found hers, and he claimed her mouth. Desire surged through him, getting stronger with every stroke. His tongue dipped into her mouth, meeting hers, licking, probing, indulging. Someone coughed.

They separated from each other, breathless, and looked to the source of the sound. Everyone in the crowd watched them, smiling, eyebrows raised.

"Well?" Solveig said.

"Well, what?" Hakon asked.

"She asked you a question. Will you marry her?"

Hakon chuckled, turned to Mia who was looking like a shy, naughty kitten. She raised her eyebrows and held out the box with the ring.

He took it. "I will marry her," he said, and a smile so bright and so beautiful spread on her face that he was blinded. The mead hall erupted in cheers and hooting and the delighted squealing of the children. Mia put the ring on his finger, and it fit perfectly.

He kissed her again, hungrily, desperately. Time stood still. Everything disappeared. All that existed was them, their souls dissolving in the kiss.

When they separated this time, Hakon looked around and people were drinking mead, talking, laughing.

Ledis sat pouting on her mother's lap, but when she saw that Hakon and Mia were free from the kissing, she beamed. "Tell us a story, Mia!"

The hall grew silent. People gave way to Hakon and Mia so that they could take their seats next to the hearth, which they did. Hakon had never felt as light, as soft, and as warm as he did now. It was as if he was swimming in the love and acceptance of everyone in the room.

Mia took his hand in hers. "Do you know the story of the boy who killed a wolf twice his size?" she asked.

Ledis shook her head, her eyes wide, serious.

Mia looked at Hakon. "Maybe it's time people knew the story of how the Beast was really born."

Hakon smiled and looked around the room. Solveig gave a barely noticeable nod.

The long winter was ahead of them with cozy evenings in front of the hearth, full of stories and legends. But they would be happy ones. Because by his side would be his wife—the love of his life, shield-maiden, healer, and time traveler.

And they would create many more stories to tell during the long winter nights of the years to come.

EPILOGUE

Lomdalen, Norway, June 21, 876 AD

Hakon wiped the blade of his battle ax with a cloth, the polished surface shining in the sunlight of the warm day. The ornate decorations on the sides of the blade depicting snarling wolves and a hunter were made of gold. Hakon had never seen anything so beautiful, except Mia. And Ulf, his five-moon-old son. The ax was his wedding gift from the whole village, and Hakon's eyes burned with gratitude and appreciation.

The ceremony was about to begin, the village buzzing with activity around him. On a meadow nearby, tables were being set to accommodate five hundred people—every single person from the village, plus the guests: King Brunn, Jarl Rafr, Jarl Vefuss, and their men. Among the guests was also the real Princess Arinborg, who stood by Jarl Rafr's side.

Rafr had taken a liking to her when she had shown up at the allies' assembly almost a year ago. Even though she had fancied Hakon when she had thought they were about to wed, her feelings had not run deep. When the allies had killed Nyr—who had insisted on attacking despite arriving too late to win back his land—Brunn had taken on responsibility for her and her sisters. She had gotten to know Rafr better throughout the winter when she had lodged with Brunn at the borg. And at the end of winter, Rafr had asked for her hand. Brunn had agreed, and the couple was happily married now.

Not as happy as Hakon and Mia though.

Hakon was satisfied with his work on the polishing and hung the ax on his belt with pride. His people had given him a gift worthy of a king.

And he felt like one.

He stood up, inhaling the scent of the upcoming feast: grilled meat, smoked fish, and cooked vegetables. Musicians played music on a lyre, a flute made of a cow's horn, and a jaw harp to entertain the guests before the ceremony and the feast.

He wished Mia and Ulf were with him so that he could share the lightness that expanded his chest like a wind-filled sail. He had not seen her since this morning because she was being prepared, and he already missed her.

But a few hours of waiting were worth it. He was about to claim her as his for the rest of their lives.

Hakon straightened his tunic, which had been made specially for the wedding. It was the color of grass burned by a long, warm summer—between green and gold. Mia said it was similar to the color of his eyes. The edges of the tunic were embroidered with a golden thread in ornate patterns. He had wanted to wear the special wedding attire for the day he would remember until the day he died.

If only to think that a year ago, he had barked at Solveig to stop the preparations for the feast.

This year, he was ready to bark so that they would hurry.

He did not need to, though. Mia made sure everything ran as smoothly as a ship.

Oda, with Ulf on her hip, approached Hakon, little Mette walking by her side with her first unsure steps. Frogeir and Torfi walked next to her.

When Ulf saw Hakon, he stretched his little arms towards him and yelled with the biggest smile on his face, "Ay!"

Hakon's chest filled with love as he took his son in his arms. His hair was the color of young honey, just like his mother. On his left temple, he had a birthmark. Not as big a one as Hakon's, just the size of Hakon's thumbnail, in the form of a heart. Neither Mia nor Dan had anything like that. Only Hakon.

The day Ulf was born, Hakon knew it was the mark of a blessing, not a curse. Because only someone blessed by the gods could be as lucky as he. The villagers agreed and treated Ulf like a little prince.

And they had named him after Hakon's father. "I love the name," Mia had said. "It's strong and beautiful. I think your mother would have approved. Ulf Hakonsson."

Naming the child he loved after the father who had feared him was the final act of forgiveness for Hakon. He would no longer allow himself to be consumed with anger and resentment. He would honor his father's memory by loving and having pride in his own son.

"Solveig says you are to go to the meadow," Oda said. "The lady is ready and soon to come."

Hakon's heart thumped so hard he thought it would break through his ribcage. "Good," Hakon said. "Frogeir, Torfi, call everyone who is not there to go to the meadow."

The men nodded and went to do as he asked. Oda stretched her arms to take Ulf, but Hakon shook his head. "I'll take him."

While Hakon walked through the village, Ulf was playing with his father's nose. "Your mother dressed you very well," Hakon said, while Ulf clenched his nostrils and laughed. Hakon looked over Ulf's tunic which was a tiny version of his. "Such a small boy, and yet a man."

Hakon and Ulf arrived at the meadow, which swarmed with people. There was a small army of cheerful, already slightly drunk men and women who were talking and laughing. Some were dancing. It was a wedding.

Under Mia's orders, the carpenter had built a wooden arch that was now covered with white flowers, and a white linen cloth, like a path, lay on the ground. Solveig stood under the arch, and Hakon, with Ulf, took his place next to her. King Brunn, Jarl Rafr, and Jarl Vefuss stood in the first honorable row, and behind them, people who Hakon knew were loyal and supportive. Children of the village, including Ledis, all free of whooping cough, were giddy with excitement. It was the best crowd he could wish for to marry the woman he loved. It had been worth the wait in order that everyone could make it.

They were talking and drinking mead from horns, servant girls and thralls going around the meadow to serve the drinks. But then everyone shushed, and Hakon's breath caught in his throat.

Mia was coming.

Hakon gave Ulf to Oda and watched the crowd split like ice under a skate. She was walking down the white linen path, and all nine worlds of Yggdrasil stopped moving.

She was not just beautiful. She was divine. She was the gates to Valhalla. Her white dress fell down her figure like a waterfall. Her hair was in a braided crown like a Norse woman's, and there were white flowers in it. And her face…he could die by just looking at her beaming smile. She was light. She was spring. She was life.

When she stood in front of him and put her hands in his, he felt as if he was about to fly high into the air like a dragon. He was one with the world, with the gods, and with the most important person.

Her.

Mia had asked that they not do the ritual of sacrificing a goat for Freyja, and she had discussed with Solveig the speech for the ceremony, which would combine some wedding traditions from her time and Hakon's time.

Solveig coughed and began.

"Dearly beloved," she said, and chuckled. Mia laughed, too, as though it was a private joke. "No. Not that. We knew Mia as Princess Arinborg first," Solveig said, and nodded to the princess who cocked her head. People chuckled. "And these two already were wed, almost exactly a year ago. But they were different people. Mia was Arinborg and Hakon was the Beast. What they have, what they overcame together, and what they became in the end is love. Love that crosses time. Love that crosses destinies. Love that conquers all."

Mia's eyes filled with tears, her lips trembled. "I did not ask her to say that," she whispered to Hakon.

He squeezed her hands in response, it was the only thing he could do, as Solveig's words rang true in his heart.

"Now, Hakon, before the gods and before men, what do you swear to Mia?"

Hakon's throat was so thick from emotion, he could barely breathe. "I give my oath to you, Mia, that I will never mistake you for anyone else." She laughed at that, happily, and the crowd echoed her. "I give you my oath that my whole being—body and soul—are yours. I will shield you from harm like a mountain. I will praise you like a nightingale. And I will go through time every day if I need to find you and bring you back home. I will love you until my last breath because I do not know how else to live. I will be your husband and my heart will beat for you until it stops."

He was sinking into her green eyes like a swimmer diving into a warm ocean.

"Hakon Ulfsson," Mia said. "I swear that I will be your wife, in every sense of the word. I came to you from another time, first by chance, then because I could not take another breath without you. To be together, we had to travel through time and negotiate with the destiny. You took in my son, Ulf, and accepted him as your own."

She paused, and her eyes shone with special meaning. Then she leaned towards him and whispered, "And now, I will give you a child to love that is of your flesh and blood."

Hakon glanced down at her flat stomach. The world suddenly heated up like boiling water. "What? You are—"

She nodded with a smile from ear to ear. "It's still very early, but I am." She straightened and continued in a louder voice, "And I promise, if destiny will allow—" She glanced at the crowd, and Hakon followed her gaze. With a shock, he saw the Norn in a Norsewoman's clothes. "If destiny will allow, I will give you many, many more. I love you more than life itself. I promise to be your partner, your wife, and your friend in this marriage—the marriage of time."

Hakon did not think his chest could fit in any more air, any more feelings, but it did. It grew, and expanded, and he was now pure light and pure love.

"In front of the gods, and in front of men, Hakon and Mia, you are now husband and wife," Solveig said.

The crowd erupted in cheers, but they faded away as Hakon swept Mia into his arms and kissed her, dissolving in love. And he knew that even Valhalla did not feel as good as his wife's kiss.

VIKING'S BRIDE

THANK you for reading VIKING'S BRIDE. I hope you loved Mia and Hakon's story. Find out what happens next when the Norns send Rachel through time to meet her soulmate Kolbjorn in VIKING'S LOVE.

A TIME-TRAVELING THIEF. A Viking warrior. She is his enemy. He is her captor. One night of passion could destroy them or set them both free.

READ VIKING'S LOVE now >

"Such a mesmerizing time travel romance story."

SIGN-UP FOR MARIAH STONE'S Newsletter:
http://mariahstone.com/signup

FEELING LIKE A BILLION DOLLARS?

And the Norns are sending people to the future, too. If you haven't read Channing and Ella's story yet, be sure to pick up AGE OF WOLVES. And yes, we will meet some of our favorite characters here again...

There's more to tattooed billionaire, Channing Hakonson,

than detective Ella O'Conner could have ever imagined—something mystical and ancient.

READ **AGE OF WOLVES** now >

 "Great twists and turns. I just couldn't stop reading!"

OR STAY in the Viking Age and read an excerpt from **VIKING'S LOVE**.

❄

CHICAGO, September 2018

RACHEL SAT on a bench on sunlit Navy Pier, watching her mother and her brother walk away. And despite the warmth of the day, the ice in her bones expanded. Her mom's arm was wrapped around James's broad shoulders for support.

Kendra had become a shadow of the vibrant, radiant artist she'd been six years ago. Her auburn hair had turned mousy, her rainbow-hued wardrobe replaced by washed out T-shirts and sweatpants, her body as thin as a match, her skin white and clammy. The only daily goal her mom had was to live till the next morning.

The doctor's appointment that morning had shaken Rachel to the core. "We found a cancerous tumor in your left kidney's renal tissue, Kendra," Dr. Khatri had said. "With end-stage renal disease, you could continue to survive on dialysis as you have for the last few years, but since cancer has come into the picture... I'm truly sorry, but my prognosis is that you have at most six months to live. If you don't get a kidney transplant, that's the best we can hope for."

Rachel's body temperature must have dropped a couple of degrees. "How does she get a kidney?" she'd asked.

"Since we know that your children's kidneys are not suitable, you need to join the transplant waiting list. The surgery and medication would come to about two hundred thousand dollars. Since you don't have insurance, there's nothing we can do even if there is a donor—unless you can raise the funds required."

Rachel's fingertips found a snag in the bench's lacquered wooden panels, and a sharp stab of pain brought her back to the present moment. She pulled out the splinter and released a long, shaky breath. Lake Michigan glittered in the bright sun, blinding passersby, but Rachel stared into space. A soft breeze carried the faint scents of fresh popcorn and cinnamon pretzels.

They had come to Navy Pier after the hospital to distract themselves and think about a solution, but desperation had clung to them like a second skin. Soon, Mom had gotten too warm and James had taken her home.

Rachel had told them she needed to go to work soon, and it didn't make sense to go all the way back to the suburbs.

The truth was, waitressing was the last thing on her mind. After six years of fear, of waiting for a miracle, and of shattered hope, Rachel's personal apocalypse breathed down her neck.

The day when the person she was closest to in this world would be gone. Eleven years ago, she had lost the one person who had always made her feel safe and protected—her dad. He had not died, though. Worse.

He'd left.

Rachel remembered how her whole body had ached with the pain of loss. She'd only been eleven years old, but that was when she'd started guarding her heart. Because if anything like that happened to her again, she was afraid she might not recover.

Like if she lost her mother.

Except, this time, Rachel could stop it from happening. All she needed was $200,000. She groaned inwardly at the seeming impossibility of it.

She sure couldn't make that waitressing. And she wouldn't pin her hopes on winning the lottery.

The chatter of three old ladies—who must have sat down beside her on the bench while she was lost in thought—made Rachel glance to her right.

"Are you all right, sweetheart?" one of the ladies asked. All three stared at her, knitting frozen in their hands. The three of them looked similar, as if they were sisters. Just the color of their clothes was different: lilac, salad green and baby blue.

Rachel cleared her throat. It had been a long time since anyone had asked if she was all right. "I'm fine."

The lady sitting closest to her studied her from behind round spectacles. "You don't look fine to me, though." She had a European accent. German? "Sometimes, life gives you an answer and you just need to act. You have no idea what adventure lies ahead of you."

She and the other two exchanged meaningful smiles and began gathering their knitting into their baskets.

"Thanks," Rachel muttered, bewildered. Who said those things to a complete stranger?

Or had Rachel heard her wrong?

The lady winked at Rachel and all three walked away.

Gold glittered on the bench next to her. The sun reflected from it and hurt her eyes for a moment. Squinting, she glanced sideways at the source of the glimmer.

A golden spindle sat next to her on the bench, looking like

something straight out of a fairy tale. What was that children's story, *Sleeping Beauty* or something? Rachel turned her head a little to see better.

The spindle had very sharp edges, almost as thin as needles. It was hard to believe this was actually gold, but years spent watching her mother work in the jewelry smithy had trained her eye to know a precious metal when she saw one. The shiny surface was engraved with unending, wavy patterns, interwoven branches of trees, beasts with open jaws and sharp teeth. *Viking* came to mind.

Rachel swallowed, sweat prickled her nape, and her hand shot to the silver necklace that her mom had made when she was born. Touching the necklace always gave her comfort in times of stress. It had a unique, simple but delicate chain, and on an oval pendant, engraved in elegant handwriting, "Rachel."

Had the ladies left the spindle behind? She almost got to her feet, ready to run after them and give it back.

But something stopped her. She could take it, and no one would know. It looked like it weighed at least ten ounces. Ten ounces of gold!

Her mind raced, making calculations. Last time she checked for her mom, gold was around $1,200 per ounce. Times ten, that was $12,000!

She was not seriously thinking about stealing! She had been honest her whole life, always doing the right thing. And look where that had gotten her...

The spindle sat at a comfortable enough distance...she could just reach down and take it. Rachel glanced around and saw that there was no one close enough to notice, and she could not see the old ladies at all.

If she were to do this, there would be no way back. She'd be a thief.

But the thought of losing her mother made Rachel's breath freeze. When her father left, her whole being had hurt—every cell, every hair, every eyelash. Losing her mother would be the end of Rachel.

Rachel shifted closer to the spindle. Her heart beat as if someone tapped a wooden mallet against her chest. She was soaked through from sweat.

Her hand crawled towards the spindle. She could almost feel the cool metal despite the sun.

"God, help me," she whispered. And with a sinking stomach, she covered the spindle with her hand and yanked it under her jacket.

But as soon as she touched the metal, the world around her disappeared. Her head spun like laundry in a washing machine, her skin hurt, the hair on her whole body stood up, and something sucked her in, as if a tornado had descended just for her.

Through terror and panic, a thought came: *Is this my punishment? Am I dying?*

And then there was nothing.

Keep reading VIKING'S LOVE.

Also by Mariah Stone

MARIAH'S TIME TRAVEL ROMANCE SERIES

- Called by a Highlander
- Called by a Viking
- Called by a Pirate
- Fated

MARIAH'S REGENCY ROMANCE SERIES

- Dukes and Secrets

VIEW ALL OF MARIAH'S BOOKS IN READING ORDER

Scan the QR code for the complete list of Mariah's ebooks, paperbacks, and audiobooks in reading order.

GET A FREE MARIAH STONE BOOK!

Join Mariah's mailing list to be the first to know of new releases, free books, special prices, and other author giveaways.

freehistoricalromancebooks.com

ENJOY THE BOOK? YOU CAN MAKE A DIFFERENCE!

Please, leave your honest review for the book.

As much as I'd love to, I don't have financial capacity like New York publishers to run ads in the newspaper or put posters in subway.

But I have something much, much more powerful!

Committed and loyal readers.

If you enjoyed the book, I'd be so grateful if you could spend five minutes leaving a review on the book's **sales page.**

Thank you very much!

ACKNOWLEDGMENTS

There are several people who have helped this book to see the light of day. THANK YOU:

Laura Barth, my amazing editor, who helped me get through the challenging process of writing this book, although I almost stopped—twice.

My husband who supports me no matter what. My 1,5-year-old son who draws on my outlines and early drafts and reminds me that life also is about fish, flowers and helicopters —not just Vikings.

My loyal, wonderful readers and the best ARC team in the world.

People with medical background who helped me check the medical facts about whooping cough: my aunt Tatiana who is a doctor; my writer friend Nicky who has a nursing background; and Kathy C., a writer friend I met online, who gave me feedback on the scenes involving pertussis, gave me tons of information about herbal medicine, and was the one who gave me the idea about a glow-in-the-dark bracelet.

My writer friends, you know who you are.

About Mariah Stone

Mariah Stone is a bestselling author of time travel romance novels, including her popular Called by a Highlander series and her hot Viking, Pirate, and Regency novels. With nearly one million books sold, Mariah writes about strong modern-day women falling in love with their soulmates across time. Her books are available worldwide in multiple languages in e-book, print, and audio.

Subscribe to Mariah's newsletter for a free time travel book today at mariahstone.com/signup!

- facebook.com/mariahstoneauthor
- instagram.com/mariahstoneauthor
- bookbub.com/authors/mariah-stone
- pinterest.com/mariahstoneauthor
- amazon.com/Mariah-Stone/e/B07JVW28PJ

www.ingramcontent.com/pod-product-compliance
Lightning Source LLC
Chambersburg PA
CBHW032241201125
35776CB00028B/325